TALES OF TWO DADDIES

Taboo MPREG Love Stories

PETER SCHUTES

CONTENTS

Three Hardcore Male Pregnancy Tales will titillate, but also amuse you. They'll give you pause to think: could this really happen? This is Speculative Fiction at its queerest and raunchiest.

THE BUTT BABY

Chuck and Nick, high school buddies with benefits, make a surprising mistake at a small orgy, leaving Chuck in a family way. Can these two find love enough to care for a child together?

THE THIGH BABY

Dale Clark is a bully. His victim, Jay, grows on him until they fall in love. When Jay's pregnant sister dies in a deadly car accident, the doctors have an unusual solution to keep the baby alive

THE EXPECTANT MEMBER

Milo falls for trans man Jordan and together, they make two babies at the same time: one grows in Jordan, but the other gestates in Milo's phallus! How and why it happens are just the beginning of this sordid, highly erotic tale.

THE BUTT BABY

PUBLISHER'S NOTE

This work of short erotic fiction was set in 1980 or 1981, not long before Peter's death (as much as a fictional pen name can die). The story is preposterous but has some basis in scientific fact. It is possible for an ectopic pregnancy to form in the rectum of a female. It happened exactly once, and the baby did not survive. This story, a highly aggressive form of sexual gay activism, takes place on the eve of the AIDS crisis. In many of his stories, we catch a glimpse of his own insecurities surrounding his overly large endowment. Nikolas, the overly hung character depicted in the story, is far removed from the characters we normally associate with Peter. We believe he didn't have a part in this story. It was pure fantasy. This story, almost a novella, belongs on a shelf next to Philip Roth's sexual fantasy fiction. It is not quite pornography, at least not when compared to Peter's other stories.

THE BUTT BABY

I rarely drink, smoke weed, take pills, or have extramarital gay sex. Eight months ago, at a dinner party, I did all four. My wife Clarissa had a really bad migraine and begged off at the eleventh hour. The party was at the home of my high school best friend, Nikolas. He wasn't Greek; his parents were just really bad spellers. Nikolas grew up in Van Nuys like I did. Unlike me, he didn't go to college. He got a job as a Producer's Assistant on a television pilot that failed to get picked up. Because of his nearly sociopathic charm and dashing good looks, he was promoted to producer on a sitcom that followed the lives of seven mermaid models. He ended up marrying Sirena, the tallest mermaid, and they bought a beautiful house in a crappy neighborhood near USC. Nikolas (he will not let you call him Nick) continued his upward spiral. His house quadrupled in value. A network put him in charge of "Movies of the Week," which turned out to be the wave of the future. Within a year, he was poached twice by other studios, each time doubling his already bloated salary. Throughout his climb to success, he never forgot the little people like Chuck, his high school buddy from Van Nuys. That's how I wound up at a dinner party in the Hollywood Hills in an early 1930s Spanish-style estate rumored to have once belonged to Clara Bow.

I'm Chuck. Eight months ago, I was living with my wife and daughter in a small bungalow in a seedy section of Van Nuys. I studied English in college, not Business, so of course I work in retail. I met my wife Clarissa over the perfume counter at the store where we both worked. She is a solid, practical woman. Ten years ago, we had a beautiful daughter named Patsy. She is the glue that keeps our marriage together.

So back to Nick's house (fuck it, I can call him what I want; I earned it), where the dinner party is off to an interesting start. Nick has a contraband bottle of absinthe he smuggled in from France, and he wants us all to try it. There are slotted spoons and sugar cubes. We all taste it. To me, it tastes like gasoline, but it does make lamps and sunsets glow neon. I tried to decline a second glass, but Nick put it in my hand and held it to my lips. It felt good to be the center of his attention. I told you he doesn't let people call him Nick. In high school, he had a growth spurt in 9th grade that caused his penis to double in size and width. He was bigger than most seniors. In the gym showers, he earned the nickname Nick the Dick. As reputations are wont to do, his new name traveled throughout the school. Contrary to what I believed at the time, it can be humiliating and painful to be the owner of a massive penis.

Nick used to talk to me about it in my bedroom.

"Chuck, I can't have a girlfriend. I'll never know if it's me or my cock she wants. I'll never know if she really likes me."

"Well, I like you." We were at that age where it didn't matter how it happened, you just needed to get off. It started with me gagging on his dick every afternoon and progressed to the absolute best sex of my life when Nick the Dick would fuck my ass deeply. He even used to kiss me. He appreciated me letting him practice on me.

"Chuck, you're a true friend. Thanks for letting me bone you, dude."

What I wanted to say was, "I love you. I will be your fuck buddy forever." What I said was, "Anything for a friend."

So yeah, I secretly loved Nick the Dick, but he never learned about it. I got over it.

Two glasses of Absinthe will cloud your judgment. The food was nearly ready when a joint started moving around the room. I didn't hesitate to take two tokes. It would help my appetite, I reasoned.

Sirena was a lousy cook. The chicken was underdone, the zucchini was soggy, and the rice was crunchy. Many of the others at the table agreed, but we said nothing.

For dessert, Nick had quaaludes. I took one. The party moved downstairs. Clothes came off. Nick had a huge round bed, big enough to fit eight of us. I had lost all ability to make smart decisions. I kissed strange women, fondled strange men, and watched Nikolas have intense sex with Sirena while somebody sucked my dull, average cock.

Nikolas made Sirena cum violently six or seven times. He couldn't go all the way inside because he was too long. Before he could cum. Sirena begged him to stop.

"Nikolas, stop! You're gonna tear a hole in my uterus or rub my cervix raw!"

He kissed her and said he had a backup plan.

The next thing I know, he's kissing me. His frustrated cock was covered in Sirena's Vaginal fluids from multiple orgasms; the slimy dick was already pressing against my sphincter. "Nick the Dick and Chuck the Fuck buddy. Ready to make it happen, amigo?"

I nodded. He pressed hard until my uptight asshole relaxed. He was in; it felt great.

The orgy around us had come to a stop. Everyone watched, amazed, as Nick shoved inch after inch of his slippery dick into me. It was like riding a bicycle. I knew just how to bend and turn to let that monstrous cock go balls deep.

"Chuck, I can't cum unless I kiss. Do you mind?"

"No. You can—"

Nick suffocated me with his tongue. The quaaludes were multiplying all the pleasurable sensations and muting any discomfort. Somebody handed me a smoking joint. I inhaled hard, then blew the smoke into Nikolas's hungry mouth. We both blew smoke out our noses. That weed was the kind that reduced gravity. Soon, there was nobody but me and Nick the Dick floating twenty feet above the roof of the house.

I released my locked lips and said, "I love you, Nikolas."

He didn't hear or pretended not to. "Dude, I'm gonna cum soon."

"Yes, please." Back in high school, he always dropped his load in my sigmoid colon.

"Nice." He loved that I knew what he wanted.

He picked up the pace and lengthened his strokes.

The room came back into focus. I loved the expression on Sirena's face as she watched her husband bury himself completely inside me. He couldn't do that with her. The back wall of her uterus couldn't possibly stretch enough, and she probably didn't know anything about anal sex.

But I knew about the trap door at the rear of the rectum. I'm guessing Sirena didn't. The transition from the rectum to the sigmoid colon is sort of a hook shape. If I could get Nick past it with a little twisting, it stayed open. Then he could go to town on me. It didn't close right away like the rectum did. Nikolas was taking full advantage of the trap door. Looking around at the others, I could tell they were curious about my bottomless asshole.

"Oh shit, dude, this is it."

"Do it, Nick, shoot it."

I held him close and waited. He threw his head back and yelled, "Oh shit! Oh shit! Oh Chuck, you're so fuckin' awesome, oh, oh!"

I felt a flood of jism flood my rectum and colon.

I didn't cum. I didn't need to. Having my ass filled with Nikolas's sperm had given me an internal orgasm. I was still spasming when Nikolas pulled out.

He walked to the dresser, showing off his perfect ass. He lit a cigarette. When he turned to bring me one, his cock followed and swung like a pendulum as he walked towards me in slow motion. It slapped a few inches above each knee. It was magnificent.

I was still in the prone position. I blew smoke rings while Nikolas rubbed my bottom.

"Dude, you have the best ass. What's your secret? Better yet, can you teach Sirena?"

I farted cum. Nikolas laughed. "I take it that's a no."

I smiled and took a drag.

"A magician never reveals his secrets."

2

CANCER SCARE

About a month after the party, I got sick. I lost my appetite and threw up a few times. Clarissa made me chicken soup. It helped. I wasn't running a fever. I went to the city clinic and got tested for VD. The results were all negative. I made an appointment with my primary care doctor. The nausea was unpredictable, but it was real. The doctor tested thyroid function, CBC, and a few other tests I never heard of. Everything was fine. The nausea subsided, and I was better. I decided it was some kind of cold or flu, and life went back to normal.

Two months after the first health scare, I got another. This was much worse. I was having painful gas and bloating, and the rectosigmoid junction felt like it was going to explode. I still thought Nikolas had given me some kind of Venereal Disease, especially because of the location of the pain. My doctor referred me to radiology. They took an X-ray. The results were terrifying. I had a lump the size of a lime in my sigmoid colon.

I thought of Clarissa and Patsy and what a terrible provider I was. I had a basic life, but that wouldn't see them through.

A doctor put a hand on my shoulder. "Relax. 95

cases in 100 are benign tumors. Don't pick out burial plots yet."

I tried to laugh, but it made the pain worse.

Things moved very quickly. I was transferred to oncology, where they scheduled me for an immediate surgery. They said a biopsy was not aggressive enough; they should get the lump out now.

I opted for local anesthesia and a sedative. I didn't want to go under and wake up to bad news. To do the surgery, they used the latest technology called ultrasound. That would allow them to pinpoint the location and make a clean extraction.

The ultrasound tech put a metal paddle on my abdomen. I was numb, but I bet those paddles were cold. From that moment forward, my life was a runaway school bus of dread and chaos.

The ultrasound tech motioned to the doctor. He looked and stared at me with the strangest expression. The nurse looked and shook her head.

"What!? What is it? What's wrong?"

The doctor clearly didn't want to say anything, so he looked at the nurse. She turned to the technician. The technician smiled sweetly. "It's okay. You're pregnant. It's a boy. Did you wanna see the baby?"

They may as well have given me propofol. I lost consciousness and didn't come to until I was in a private room at UCLA Hospital.

My wife was working, but she arrived, as we had planned, after her shift. She took one look at my face and started crying,

"Shh. Shh, honey, it's okay. I don't have cancer."

"What's wrong?"

"To be honest, I think I passed out, so I don't really remember." That was a lie. You never forget when they tell you you're pregnant. I wasn't ready to share that with her.

A very well-dressed Doctor in emerald cufflinks and Alden shoes entered my suite.

"Honey, let me have a moment alone with Dr..."

"Dr. Prizziti. Madam, I do need to have a word in private with your husband."

When we were alone, he laid it all out. "I'm the chief surgeon here at UCLA Med. Chuck, you have a miracle growing inside you. I'm sure you realize that."

I nodded. What could I say?

"The clinical term for it is ectopic pregnancy. It has only ever happened in women, or at least that we know of. You are the world's first man to carry an ectopic fetus to 12 weeks."

"Are there any other men who've carried a fetus at all?"

"It's suspected to have happened, but it was not viable. Usually, they occur in the lower rectum, where they cannot survive. They would just get expelled with feces. Yours, however, is in the rectosigmoid junction. It is the perfect environment for a fetus to attach and survive."

I was dreading having to tell them how it happened. It could only have been Nikolas. But... "Doctor, how can a baby get made there at all? Do I have ovaries?"

The doctor smiled. "When this happens in women, we know, it is because the man has somehow stimulated her to release an egg or eggs. Usually, it is from vigorous sex that rubs the cervix. He then inserts his penis, with the egg on it, into the anal canal and fertilizes it there."

"That sounds right." I didn't mean to say it out loud.

"Please, tell me what you know. If it is recorded in a medical journal, your identity will remain protected."

I sighed. "It must be my high school fuck buddy Nikolas. He had a party three months ago, and, well..."

"Details will help immensely."

"Nikolas is hung like a horse. His wife asked him to stop because her cervix was sore. He could never fully penetrate her due to his size. So he immediately comes to me, his old pal, and fucks me. His cock was covered in, uh, vaginal fluids."

"Sounds like we know who the father and mother are," In my entire life, I never once imagined a doctor saying something so bizarre to me.

Clarissa knocked, "May I come in now?" I looked at the doctor and shook my head.

"Just a few more minutes, I assure you that your husband is healthy and disease free." Clarissa made an impatient snort and left us to continue our discussion.

"What are my choices? Do I have to tell everyone?"

"You can terminate right now. It's already a huge medical breakthrough. But you don't have to."

I thought about the little spawn of Nikolas inside me. I could never make him love me. Maybe this would bring us closer together? Isn't that crazy lady thinking?

"Dr. Prizziti, if I choose to continue, won't I die?"

"I have seen the ultrasound images. You will need a temporary colostomy. It isn't as bad as it sounds. We also need to encourage the fetus to expand into your Sigmoid colon and not into the rectum, so we would be sealing that off. Your sigmoid colon can painlessly expand enough to hold a toddler." I thought about Nick the Dick coming inside my sigmoid colon, and I grew hard under the covers,

"Yeah, I know it can handle very large objects."

3

UPHEAVAL

Upon hearing the news. Clarissa left me and took our beloved Patsy with her. Unlike Sirena, she felt that fucking around with your old high school buddy was cheating. I couldn't persuade her otherwise.

Despite all the promises, news of my condition leaked to the press. I had been waiting to tell Nikolas, so it was a nasty surprise when he phoned me up.

"Dude, what the fuck?"

"Hi, Nikolas. So...strange, right?"

"You are a fucking freak, dude. Sirena's freaking out; she wants the baby because it's her eggs. You don't know how much trouble you caused me."

"Me? You got me pregnant. How is this on me?"

"Fucking a dude in the ass. It is in no way my fault."

I have a terrible sense of timing, "Nikolas, I always wanted to be more than just friends; now you're the father of my baby. It could mean so much."

"So much fucking child support. Chuck, fuck you. I know you fucking think you love me, but it's not true, and you know why not?"

"No."

"Because I don't love you." He slammed down the phone. Well, isn't that just like a man? Tears poured out of my eyes. I heard the colostomy bag fill with stinky brown liquid. God, I would give anything to be able to fart.

I don't know how to explain my behavior. I needed to drown my sorrows in sperm. I went to the Roman Holiday, a bathhouse for old people. I figured my colostomy bag wouldn't gross out the seniors. I lay face down on a mattress with the door propped open. One after another, men of all shapes and sizes came into my room and left semen inside me; I know what you're thinking. It won't hurt the baby. My rectum was already sewn shut to make the sigmoid colon a hermetic environment. My ass was always clean. I just douched out the sperm from the night before, and I was ready for another round. It kept my rectum from drying out, and it was better than drugs. It killed all the pain, drowned all the shame, and made me happy to be alive, three minutes at a time.

The problems began after I landed an agent who sold my story to Warner Brothers. They made me go on a press junket around the country to drum up initial interest in my story. In each new town, I found a dismal bathhouse for seniors and collected their semen. It worked for some reason. The first problem came in Houston. I had to do a television appearance on Saturday and a Monday morning radio show. Saturday night at the baths, people saw me walking to my room. They pointed and whispered. Shit, they knew who I was. I lay face down on my mattress, only to receive a tap on my shoulder,

"Out."

It was the manager.

"Why? I paid admission like everyone else,"

"You should not put that baby at risk, and I won't stand for it,"

"But the baby is sealed—"

"Get out, Chuck, or I'll call the cops."

It was creepy enough that he knew I had a baby up my butt, but when he called me by name, I realized what a mistake I had made. Sure, the money was fantastic. The fame was going to destroy me.

Traveling the country was stressful for several reasons. First, the air travel wasn't good for the baby. In fact, it was far worse than the shifty shit I was doing in the bathhouses. Like I already said, that baby was sealed off from anything going on in my rectum. Unfortunately, snap judgments were more powerful than my carefully worded anatomical explanations.

New York was the next leg of my undoing. My agent arranged an innocent talk show appearance, but I was met with a mob of anti-gay protesters in the audience. Wanda Waters, the host, stood up and told the audience that unless they could be respectful, then they could just leave. More than half the audience left. I felt a moment of relief.

Then it went something like this:

"What do you attribute all this hatred and protest to, Chuck?"

"Wanda, I'm not sure. I think there is a visceral reaction when nature is turned on its head."

"Some are calling your unborn child Antichrist."

"Well, if he's my child, I doubt he will have such a winning personality." The audience didn't laugh at my self-deprecating humor. Nobody reads their Bibles. I hate having to explain my jokes. "The Bible says that the Antichrist will be universally loved and respected."

Wanda nodded absently, already formulating her next question. I was parched; I grabbed the water glass.

"Are the rumors true that you are endangering the baby by having unprotected sex with dozens of men every night?" I had no intention of soaking Wanda with my mouthful of water; it just happened. She wiped my drink from her face and leaned back towards the control room. "Roll footage."

On the screen, someone, some coward, narrated as he followed me to the Flex Spa in New Orleans.

"That is Chuck, the world's first pregnant man. He is going into a place where the gays do sex."

He waited in line behind me and paid his entry fee.

There was a lot of blurred-out footage, with my face popping up once every so often. The final shot showed me face down, being sodomized by a mass of giant pixels.

The audience booed. I tried to explain.

"You don't get it. I'm not endangering the baby. They sealed it away from my rectum, so it's perfectly safe."

My voice couldn't be heard over the shouts and jeers.

It must have been all the hormone injections. I put my head in my hands and cried. I cried so hard and so loud that Wanda felt compelled to hold me. The audience quieted long enough for me to speak in my own defense.

"I cleared it with the doctor. It's sealed off. It's like an armpit."

Wanda started taking questions from the audience. A man with spiked hair stood.

"Man, what do your parents think of all this?"

I wanted to attack him and ask what his parents thought of his choice of hairstyles, but I kept my cool.

"They're dead, but if they were alive, I know they would be very proud of me. I'm risking my life for science. Some day, men will carry babies to term without any fuss whatsoever."

A freckle-faced woman stood up and straightened her skirt and blouse. "I think it's disgusting what you're doing."

I was not going to let her get away with a lame-ass ad hominem attack. "Can you specify the things that disgust you?"

"I mean, gross, you did it in the butt. And now you're doing it in the butt all the time...while you're pregnant. Eew."

"What's your point?"

She fidgeted. "It's against the Bible."

I didn't back down. "Science is against the Bible too. I see you're wearing hairspray and a pair of nylon stockings. Is God angry with you?"

There were murmurs of agreement. I was winning the crowd over. But Wanda wasn't much of an ally.

"How many men here would have anal sex if they knew they might become pregnant? Let's have a show of hands....Nobody? What if you knew you wouldn't get pregnant. That would be fun, yeah? Hold those hands up. Oh, there aren't any. "

I admit my next step was a real gaffe. "Wanda, statistics show that over half of these men have had it at least once in their life. Nobody wants to admit it."

She threw me in front of a speeding Mack Truck. "What do you think, men? A little 'woo-woo in the hoo-hoo?' I thought not." The remainder of the segment sounded like an audience at a boxing match.

Men are such hypocrites. After the show, a half dozen asked to meet up in my hotel room. When I was able to ascertain that they were not axe murderers, I gave them my info. Tonight, the baths would come to me. But the majority of the men and women I talked to after the show were hostile, defensive, and very disturbed. Still, I maintained a calm and pleasant demeanor. It was the best defense against their irrational attacks. At the stage door, there was a lone man waiting for me. It was Nikolas.

"What are you doing here?"

"It was in the TV Guide, so I flew out. I didn't know where you were."

"Does Sirena know you're in New York?"

"She thinks I'm at a film festival in Italy."

I was not unhappy to see him, but I was still angry.

"I lost everything because of you and your wife's vaginal fluids. Are you here to try and take something more?"

He shook his head.

"Look, Chuck, you're going to ride a wave of notoriety, and then the money is going to dry up. I don't want my son or daughter living in poverty. Will you let us have the child after it's born?"

"The 'it' you are referring to is a boy, and he is mine."

Nikolas brightened up. "You mean we have a son?" For a brief moment, I felt like the 'we' meant that he was sharing responsibility. "Sirena will be psyched." No, "we" meant him and his egg-drop wife. It hurt terribly to be all alone in this. I wasn't a "we". Well, my future son and I were. Patsy would have a little brother. If Clarissa had anything to do with it, she would never let them meet, but the law had something different to say.

I felt a rumble in my gut. It was coming from my sigmoid colon. The baby kicked!

Silently, I put Nikolas's hand on my belly. We both felt a kick. His eyes went wide with amazement.

"Chuck, is that our...is that my...let me ask again. Is that the baby I put in you?"

I nodded. It felt so good to feel even the most tenuous connection to him. I put my hand over his. He withdrew. When he saw my eyes fill with tears, he put his hand over mine.

"Chuck, this is beyond fucked up. I mean, we're in uncharted waters. I don't know how to be a good friend to you, but I want to be."

"Tell Sirena to back off."

"Chuck, you can't raise a baby. Not on your own. Please let us have the kid."

I was about to attack, but he retraced his words. "I

mean, please let us share the responsibility of raising our son. The son I made with you. Our son."

The tears came too easily. My nipples hurt when I hugged him, but I just held him close and let him stroke my hair. It was New York; nobody cared about two affectionate men. Not like they do in the South.

"I'm meeting some reporters in my room in a little while. I wish you could see the incredible view. But I don't want reporters near you, Nikolas."

So far, I have successfully kept Nikolas's name and identity a secret. But of course, there were no reporters coming. It was the lecherous gathering of male Wanda Waters audience members who wanted to cum inside a pregnant man.

"Can I come by late? Like two in the morning.?"

I hated lying and telling Nikolas I didn't want to see him. I had no idea how late that party was going to last. Nikolas had a strange ability to tell what was really going on.

"If you're having another one of your cum orgies, I'm happy to add my glaze to your donut."

I pushed him away, trying to be offended rather than amazed and guilty. It didn't work.

"Reporters don't have press junkets in hotel rooms, not even for Stevie Nicks."

In the end, I invited Nikolas to my little orgy.

"You can come, but I want you for breakfast."

❄ 4 ❄

GLAZED DONUTS

I had Nikolas to myself for a couple of hours. No one would show up until 11 pm. We ordered room service. Nikolas wasn't impressed with the room. He clearly had seen better. While we waited for the food to arrive, I lay on the bed and let him stroke my tummy. He put his ear there but didn't hear anything. Every few minutes, he would inhale suddenly, then tickle my tummy where he felt it. It was probably the most intimate experience I ever had with him since we first started fucking in high school.

At 11 pm, the phone rang. It was one of the six creepy audience members. I didn't care about who they were or what they looked like. I just needed to be a cum hole to numb the loneliness. But now that Nikolas was here, it felt hollow and useless. I only ever wanted this sloppy, dirty sex to forget about him.

"Nikolas, he's on his way. He mustn't suspect who you are. You'd better start fucking me." He nodded. Some hotel lotion was all he needed to get started. I sighed with pleasure when he put it in me. He hit the back porch, but the screen door was locked up tight. I couldn't let him in all the way; the doctors had sewn it shut. He put his fist around the base of his cock, and that prevented the painful bottoming out.

"Dude, it's closed. You feel like Sirena."

"I feel way better than Sirena, and you know it."

One by one, the old trolls from the audience arrived. Nikolas was doing a masterful job of fucking me. Two men were intimidated by his huge cock; they left. The rest waited patiently for their chance to spill their seed inside The Pregnant Man.

Nikolas finished with a single painful full-throttle thrust into the sealed end of my rectum. I felt hot cum struggling to move forward, only to squirt backward. It was the first of many loads that night. Nobody but Nikolas had ever hit the seam. I couldn't wait for the baby to be born so I could have him all the way inside me. If he ever would. A fat man with a painfully fat chode was giving my sphincter a real stretch. He hurt, but only because of how dilated I became. When he pulled out or fell out accidentally, I felt the hotel air-conditioning in my hole. I must have been gaping wide open.

Nikolas cut in line more than a few times. He wanted to mark his territory. Nobody knew he was the man whose sperm had made me pregnant. Only I got to revel in the perversity of having him dump multiple loads into my blind rectum. I was so tired I passed out.

In the morning, Nikolas was still in my bed. He had wrapped his arms around me in his sleep. I guess it was something that he did with Sirena, and it really wasn't meant for me. But then he opened his eyes and kissed me. Then he really kissed me, and then we both got too excited to go to breakfast. He put his dick inside me and pushed his way through the congealed jelly that had been hot drippy cum last night. He was so turned on it only took him a minute to add his fresh broth to the stew. I asked Nikolas to order breakfast room service, then I went to the bathroom and used the bidet to wash away a dozen loads of baby gravy.

We switched on the morning news. I groaned. The

lead story was about last night's show. The image that caused me deep dread was the freckle-faced girl saying"...Now you do it in the butt all the time...while you're pregnant. Ewe!"

It cut to a faraway shot of me kissing Nikolas outside the stage door. "Mystery man in Chuck's life? What is he hiding that we all should know?"

Nikolas sat stock still.

"Nikolas, it's dark; no one can tell it's you."

The TV further destroyed me. "Our sources say this man is a long time friend. Could he be the father of Chuck's baby?"

I thought maybe I was having a bad dream, but the smell of fresh sex on the sheets was too real.

Nikolas paced in circles. "Fuck, fuck, fuck!. What the fuck! Chuck, if this is your doing, I swear I will punch that baby right out of you."

I held my hands up. "You just showed up. I had no idea there were paparazzi."

The video of the dickwad following me into Flex in New Orleans was added to the blitz of negative coverage.

When room service came, I told Nikolas to stay in the bathroom. I had a plan.

We devoured our eggs, sausage, grilled tomatoes, toast, and hash browns. The room service cart was exactly as I had hoped. It was like one of those media carts from school, covered with a long tablecloth.

Nikolas climbed to the bottom, and I rolled it to the elevator. It was empty when it opened. I signaled for Nick to get out. When he was in the elevator, I mouthed, "I love you." He grinned, but he didn't say it back.

My publicist canceled the tour and suggested I fake an almost miscarriage at UCLA Hospital. She wanted me to go on the record as saying that I had engaged in disgusting behavior, and this near miscarriage showed me how bad it was for the baby, and from now forward, I was going to be a saint or some such nonsense. It was humiliating lies, but I told them.

To make it real, I stayed in a bed with a view of the ocean and greeted reporters one by one. With my baby "at risk" they were much more sympathetic. I wanted to spit in their faces when I denounced my 'disgusting behavior' but that wouldn't have the intended effect. The follow-up questions were designed to make me feel ashamed and lose myself, like a woman of ill repute. They worked.

"So, once this is behind you, will you go back to the life?"

"The life?"

"Selling yourself to men."

"I didn't sell myself! I gave it away. There's a difference."

"So you're going to take all comers, so to speak." Oh, she thought that was clever. How rich, how amusing.

Every interview followed that template. I am so lucky to still have my baby after the terrible things I put it through. Thank goodness you have seen the error of your ways.

On the Nightly News, there was a story about a Lebanese man who was pregnant. He would have the best health care the nation had to offer. He was considered a national hero. A few weeks later, he was thrown in jail when it came to light that he had committed sodomy to be impregnated. The six-week fetus died due to deplorable conditions. The man pooped it out in a prison toilet. What is it with The Middle East? How did they think he got sperm in his asshole? A toilet seat?

The Ayatollah in Iran proclaimed a fatwa on me. I was perverting the glory of Allah. If I could argue back, I would tell him that Allah had created the loophole that landed me in this mess. I didn't choose it. Oh, but I did choose sodomy. Death to the infidels! If those Muslims knew how good it feels to get fucked in the butt, I'll bet they'd find a way to allow it.

India was the next country to produce a man with an ectopic pregnancy. His story resembled mine. He was very high on Hindu Khush bud when he "accidentally" let his friend have intercourse with him after sex with his wife. Because it was an "accident," it made everything forgivable in the eyes of the several hundred religions practiced in India that were all poised to condemn him. A team of Indian doctors appeared in my room one day. They examined me in places no doctor should look without permission. Endoscopies, measurement and weighing of my genitals, ultrasound, and a brain scan. They measured the Ph of my rectum. They took vial after vial of blood to check hormone levels, minerals, vitamins, electrolytes, and things that are probably only recognized in Ayurveda. They were extremely grateful and returned to the man at home, prepared to make him the second man to bring a baby to term. Unfortunately, the surgery for the colostomy happened in unsanitary conditions. The resulting infections created complications, and the poor man died of sepsis. I envied him at times but pitied him more often.

BLINDSIDED

It was nearly five months when I saw Nikolas again. He came to my room in full daylight, where any gossip columnist could have spotted him.

"Nikolas, it's so great to see you!" then whispered, "Are you nuts? You're going to be exposed!"

Nikolas shrugged. He seemed pretty pleased with himself.

"How's Sirena?"

"We split. She took the house and our joint money. I got the accounts in the Cayman Islands, so fuck her."

I remembered how much it hurt when Clarissa left, so I held his hand and asked, "Are you okay?"

"Dude, I am like perfect. I am the father of a boy, the most extraordinary boy in the world, whose other father is my best friend."

"Are you sure you're okay?"

He laughed. "Chuck, you're so afraid. Live! Be happy! It's good for our baby." He said 'our' and meant it this time.

"Why did you decide to call it quits?"

"Sirena wouldn't let up about her fucking eggs giving her custody of your baby. I wanted to protect you, so I told her that I would divorce her and give her the house and all of our bank accounts (in the US) if she would drop it. She had to sign a contract and everything. Your baby...our baby is legally shielded from her.

I was touched that he chose to protect me over his wife. "Where does that leave us?" I was perplexed.

"Why do you think I'm so fucking happy? Dude, you know I have loved you forever!" In hindsight, it was probably a bad idea, but he made me cry happy tears when he jumped up on the hospital bed and shouted at the top of his lungs, "I love this man. We're having a baby! Our baby!"

I actually felt weird about it. Somewhere in the back of my mind, I thought I would win Clarissa back and take Patsy to soccer practice. He hadn't asked me; he just assumed. Okay, he assumed correctly, but it still would have been nice to be consulted prior to this bizarre proclamation of love.

The hormones they gave me were getting stronger week by week. Nikolas's happy announcement made tears well up in my eyes. Then I started to really cry. Nikolas gave me his handkerchief, and I lost all control. I sobbed for what seemed like three days but was really only fifteen minutes. "Oh, god, Nikolas. I've been so alone!"

"Does that mean you'll say yes if I ask you to be my lover?" He was pushy.

I nodded. I couldn't speak through the sobs.

He hugged me hard, then drew back.

"What's that?" he asked, pointing to my hospital gown at chest level. Two wet spots were spreading from my nipples. I felt warm liquid puddling in my belly button. It was milk.

Doctors pushed Nikolas aside to capture and test the milk. It was unclear if it was fit for human consumption. When the doctors left the room, Nikolas asked me to nurse him. It was such a crazy day; I chose to be happy about the request. He buried his face in my nipple and slurped the nourishment from my breast. It felt sexual, and I got a boner. Nick the Dick got a boner too, somewhere down his pant leg. Nothing could be done. I stroked him surreptitiously, but it only made our situation worse.

After hours of nursing, hugging, and various unfulfilled sexual needs, I turned the TV on to distract us. I was pleasantly surprised by the coverage. Some sneak had recorded Nikolas's declaration of love and confession of fatherhood. Instead of eating him alive, the press praised him for stepping up and doing the right thing. Nikolas nursed me dry while I flipped between news channels. How could there be nothing unfavorable? "Love conquers all." read one of the chyrons. "Studio EVP steps up. Vows to protect Chuck." He didn't say that!

"Nikolas, how come they're treating you so well in the media?"

"I have PR people that not even the president can afford. And now, you do too."

That's all it boils down to, really, how the public perceives you.

Over the next eight weeks, as I started to show, Nick's PR people arranged interviews, charity appearances, and gay pride parades. I'm not even gay! Actually, I guess I am. I'm a man who has sex with men.

Nikolas got me out of the hospital and into private nursing care with the best OB/GYN in Hollywood. The man was utterly starstruck. We were sequestered, living in obscurity in the Alto Nido. It was the happiest time of my life. I was an expectant father, living with the man I loved since high school. Even though it left me sore, the constant sex was brilliant. It even was good for the baby. A screening revealed that the baby was healthier than when we left the hospital. Love and sex were better than vitamins.

The only problem with love and sex was the length of Nikolas's dick. He tried to hold back, but he often slipped and hit the sutures. About a week ago, I felt something was wrong. The pain near my sutures wouldn't go away. I didn't know it yet, but Nick had ruptured the seal. The baby was exposed to my rectum, and I was developing an infection. The following day, during a session of afternoon delight, I was in excruciating pain. I tried to hide it, but when Nikolas slipped and hit the seal, the stitches came loose completely. My hole was wide open. I lost a lot of blood. The last thing I remember was the doctor giving me a cocktail that put me under.

When I awoke, I saw Nikolas, Clarissa, and my little Patsy smiling down at me. Nikolas spoke the truth when he called her up and said I might die. They came in case they had to say "goodbye." Clarissa wiped back tears

As I smiled at them, I felt for the familiar lump on my belly. It was still there. Thank goodness my son - our son was still there.

Dr. Prizziti came in with a clipboard and a furrowed brow. He spoke softly just to me and Nikolas. "What did Nikolas do to you?"

"Nothing. I mean, well, we had butt sex, but you yourself said this would be okay."

"We hadn't counted on an anomaly like him. Do you realize fewer than five thousand people in the whole world can claim a dick so long?"

Nikolas beamed with pride. He said, "I always knew I was big, but that's insane!"

Dr. Prizziti interrupted. "What's insane is that your big dick tore open the rectosigmoid sutures. Your baby is exposed. And you have lost a lot of blood."

"I didn't know. How can that be wrong?"

"Chuck, you are going to lose that child. An infection surrounds him. Only his amniotic sac prevents him from becoming contaminated with your sigmoiditis."

"Can you do a Caesarian?"

The doctor shook his head. "Too risky."

"For me or for the baby?"

"Both."

"What can we do?"

Doctor Prizziti wiped his brow.

"You're going to have to stay very still for a few weeks. Your fetus is at 7 ½ months; it's too dangerous now. In your 8th month, we can try a procedure. He took his clipboard and walked out.

With hormones raging through my system, I sobbed aloud. "I don't care about me. Will our baby live?"

Patsy began crying, "Daddy, I don't want to lose you!" That caused Clarissa to grow vicious. "Jesus Christ, Chuck, look what you're doing to our daughter."

"Leave him alone!" Patsy shouted at her mother, "he's my daddy! You left but I didn't!" A hard smack to the face didn't help anything. Patsy bawled her head off.

Clarissa pulled Patsy off of me and vanished.

Nikolas shook his head. "Dude, I feel like a bonehead. I hurt you, I hurt the baby, and I may have destroyed a scientific discovery that could change life forever."

I didn't have the energy to comfort Nikolas properly. I did my best. "It takes two to do it in the butt."

It worked. Nikolas laughed and gently hugged me. "Don't move. If you need anything, any little thing, I'm right here. All night, every night."

I nodded and drifted into a dreamless sleep.

I woke in the morning to Nikolas holding steaming hot scrambled eggs to my nose. It was not an odor an expectant mother or father wants to smell. I gagged.

"Shit, I can't do anything right. What do you want."

"Orange juice."

He gave me the glass, wrapped in Saran Wrap. I unpeeled it and drank the bitter, acidic liquid.

"Ugh, what's in that?"

"I think they're giving you the same vitamins they give a woman in this situation."

"A woman with a baby up her butt?

"You know what I meant. Ha ha."

They had managed to clear away the infection. My belly was swollen with child. It was the strangest feeling. It made me have to pee every five seconds. I was also unbearably horny. Late at night, when the lights were out, I convinced Nikolas to let me blow him. I think the doctors wouldn't have liked it, but I was hungry for cum, and Nikolas was the very best provider I knew. I stayed still like they wanted, but I draped my head off the end of the bed. This allowed Nikolas to fuck me in the throat without any obstructions, so I didn't move as long as he went slow. When things got too heated, and he was about to erupt, I took the end and lovingly swallowed his semen. I had twin rivulets of cum dripping down either side of my mouth. He used his dickhead to wipe me clean. It took a while because he kept getting more man jam on my face than he was removing.

Nikolas kissed my cummy mouth and licked his lips. "Am I your favorite flavor, Chuckie?"

I nodded. "Best ass-fucker, best throat-fucker, sweetest cum: dude, you're the whole package."

He smiled. "And I've landed the softest mouth and the sweetest ass. So sweet, I fucked a baby into it."

The doctor was being a bit secretive about my upcoming birth. A few weeks before the due date, he told me what was up.

"Chuck, the infection has left only one alternative. You are going to give birth through the anal canal.

I was puzzled...what was wrong with it?

"I can handle it."

The doctor nodded. You can handle Nikolas. His baby, your baby, will be just as long but thicker than a football. Many men engage in a practice called "fisting."

I think this would be very beneficial to you and your baby.

Nikolas said, "Fisting? Gnarly."

The doctor presented a videocassette of a man in a leather swing, taking two, three, four, five fingers and then writhing in ecstasy as the man put his whole hand in. The doctor fast-forwarded over a section where the fister inserted his entire arm. "This is strictly off limits. Then, he played a section that made my jaw drop. The man in the swing moaned and shouted hoarsely while the fister inserted both hands at once, then grabbed the edges of his hole and pulled, stretching it beyond any size I ever dreamed possible. He could have put his head up there.

The doctor turned to us. "This takes many sessions to achieve. You will need to do this every night until the operation.

Nikolas asked, "What was that white cream they used?"

"Crisco," the doctor answered. We have a sterile obstetric solution that will work much better. Nikolas will need to wash both hands and wear rubber gloves."

The first session went surprisingly well. The hard part for me was to lay still while Nikolas was giving me multiple anal orgasms. Because we share such a deep connection, he was able to tell when to push me and when to hold back. He knew the nuances of my sex noises. That first time, Nick pushed his long, thick fingers against my prostate. I leaked clear jizz. A nurse wiped it away. Even with our every move being examined under a microscope, I was so turned on by Nikolas that I kept my hard-on. In the video, as I recall, the fisting bottom was soft. When Nikolas pressed his whole hand in, I sprayed cum all over the operating room. The nurse cleaned up, huffing angrily. She will never know the pleasure that brought me to that orgasm. When the anal orgasms started, I couldn't control the violent spasms. Two orderlies held down my shoulders. Nikolas and the doctor held my hips until I could not thrash and cause damage to myself or the boy living inside my poop chute.

The session ended when I had a second ejaculation that was more cum than the first. The nurse threw her hat down and walked out. Nikolas removed his hand, balled up in a fist. It hurt so bad I saw stars. But that was the goal, of course, to loosen me up for baby birthing.

On the second day, the staff took precautions that were not immediately to my liking. I was strapped tightly to the table, like a death row inmate getting a lethal injection. The nurse covered my penis with a condom. This time, Nikolas's goal was to put in one hand, remove it, and put in the other, then back to the first, and so on. The hope was that he could insert his fists into me like a boxer slowly punching a bag. Everything hurt a lot more, as it often does with anal sex on the second day. I didn't care. I got to look at Nikolas's eyes and feel him enter me over and over again. His fist by itself wasn't much bigger around than his dick. He got into the rhythm, and my eyes rolled back in my head. I came so much that the condom flew off like a rocket. The nurse struggled to put another on me. I hit her in the face. It wasn't my fault.

The straps that bound me and caused me distress earlier made me suddenly feel very safe. Nikolas was there to protect me. He was there to make my butthole into a manhole. The straps were like me showing my commitment to him. I was bound to him. It was bondage.

The session ended when Nikolas could enter and exit me five times in 15 seconds, using alternating hands. I didn't want it to end.

On the third day, we reached our goal. Nikolas put both fists inside me at the same time. I couldn't thrash, but I could scream. It was what we needed for the baby, but it hurt so bad my cock went soft.

Doctor Prizziti praised Nikolas for his expert manipulation, and he complimented me on my commitment to the cause of science.

I later learned that the mirror on the wall beside us was a viewing theater. Doctors from every nation watched while I got my hole reamed by Nikolas and his beautiful hands.

After day three, it was always the goal to get to two fists, but we extended the amount of time in small increments. It became pointless when I could easily take his hands. I could take them for hours and it didn't hurt. I might feel a little sore afterwards, but it was a tingly feeling not pain.

We had to keep my rectum sterile. The nurse would insert a dressing to protect the amniotic sac and then give me a gentle enema. One day, the female nurse didn't come. Instead, Nelson, a rough, muscular male nurse, was in charge of cleaning out my ass. He seemed nervous around me, so I figured he was straight. I kept my jokes and sarcasm to a minimum. But as the procedure ended and the doctors left us alone, he whispered in my ear. "God, I wanna fuck you."

I popped a boner immediately. Strapped to the table, I wasn't able to do anything to resist. The nurse wheeled me out of the operating room and into an empty private suite. My ass was still stretched out and slippery with obstetric lubricant. He pulled down his pants and revealed a massive tree stump of a cock. He took off his shirt, revealing a thick, muscular chest with fur descending into his pants. He was going to hurt the baby. I heaved a sigh of relief when he produced a condom. It was too slim for him. He just did that to impress me. He pulled it on, and it snapped like a party balloon.

He rubbed his crotch. "You got a big fuckin' hole.

Big enough to handle me." His weeping willow tree became a mighty oak.

"Help!" I shouted, hoping someone would come. The nurse produced a leather ball gag and popped it in my mouth, wrapping it tight around my head. I could breathe through my nose, but just barely.

I had no way to explain how dangerous this was for the baby. He was devastatingly handsome, which made the rape all the worse because I wanted it. I wanted this thick, sexy nurse to fill my dilated hole and shoot his load inside me.

"Yes!" he shouted. "Oh, man, you are perfect!" He easily shoved his beast of a cock inside me. It was long, but not long like Nikolas. He reached the general vicinity of the torn stitches, but he didn't turn any corners.

Like an animal, he rutted me, rubbing my belly and saying, "I wanna get you pregnant again. You're gonna have two babies when I'm done with you." I didn't try to talk him out of it because I couldn't. The worst part, my cock was standing at full attention, dribbling precum like it was Old Faithful.

My leaking hard cock only encouraged the nurse as he rutted me violently. "I'm gonna plant my seed in your ass. It's gonna grow." He had a fetish. He wanted to make me pregnant. Oh, how I hated myself for enjoying the whole thing. When at last, he held himself close and stopped his ceaseless fucking, I grabbed his ass to hold him closer. That was all he needed. He blew a geyser of cum into my stretched hole. I was so turned on that I shot my load in his face. He smacked me hard for that.

He held a scalpel to my throat. "One word about this, and you won't see daylight. Got me?"

I nodded.

He undid the ball gag, and I gasped in several lungfuls of fresh air.

He smiled at me. "Did you like that, mama man?"

"It was fucking amazing."

He cleaned out my hole with a gentle squeeze from a Fleet enema. I hoped it hadn't hurt the baby.

Nelson, the nurse with the elephantine cock was my nurse now. The rapes became a daily encounter following my fisting session with Nikolas. When the hospital tested the baby, he had improved since the last test before I met Nelson. It was still true that good anal sex was better than vitamins. I was cheating on Nikolas, but I had no choice, so I didn't feel guilty. Nikolas was using two hands every day now, opening me up so Nelson could play cuckoo bird and invade my nest.

About a week ago, the doctors determined that I could have the baby. Nelson wheeled me to our empty room and threatened me some more.

"Chuck, I am gonna fuck you regularly, or I will cut that baby's throat."

I was gagged, but I shook my head.

"No? What do you mean, no?"

I shrugged, so he removed the gag.

"Nelson, it's been fun. If you go to Silverlake, you will meet many men who can do what I do. I'm not the only one."

"You're the only one who's pregnant."

"Not after today."

"I want to make you pregnant."

"Soon, you can make any man pregnant. At least any man who is stretched out enough to accommodate you."

He punched me hard enough to leave a bruise, but then he wheeled me back to my room, undoing the straps.

He bowed his head and left when Dr. Prizziti came in. "Chuck, are you ready to make history?"

I smiled. "As ready as I'll ever be."

He rolled me into the ER. A team of top-notch doctors and the very best nurses surrounded me. Nikolas was right beside me. Nelson wasn't here. I was safe, for now. Once our boy was born, I would let Dr. Prizziti know what Nelson had done. Hopefully, he would get put away for a long time. I would miss his incredibly thick cock, though. He would have an interesting time in prison.

Lights came on, and I received an injection in my arm. Suddenly, I felt like I had diarrhea. My colostomy bag was filled to overflowing. The nurses changed it. But in my rectum, the need to poop was fierce. It didn't hurt, exactly, but it didn't feel like a party, either.

Nikolas saw my face and panicked.

"Doc, is he okay?"

"I'm fine, Nikolas. It hurts a little." I held his hand. "We're going to be fathers soon." I had never seen Nikolas cry. His eyes were brimming with tears. Maybe he had some of these hormones or something.

With a splash, my water broke. It leaked out of my loose hole. A doctor captured it in a plastic tray to test. Apparently, there was some question about the type of chromosome we would find in the amniotic fluid.

Dr. Prizziti flooded my rectum with sterile obstetric lubricant. I felt a mass moving from my sigmoid colon into the rectum. It was painful. This was not a place we had loosened with all those fisting sessions. It was a narrow pass, and it hurt like a motherfucker.

Somebody gave me another shot, and suddenly, the world grew fuzzy. Nikolas was still crying. I frowned at him. He's supposed to be the big man.

"Nikolas, what is it?"

"I'm just so afraid of losing you"

"Look around you. There are fewer people in Boise, Idaho, than there are doctors in this room. I promise I won't die."

Nikolas smiled at my wry humor.

I screamed a few times while our boy moved

through my rectosigmoid junction. It was far too narrow for a baby, but it was extremely flexible, and ultimately the baby made it through. Once he was in my rectum, we were in a territory well-stretched by Nikolas and Nelson. Wave after wave of peristalsis pushed him to my anal canal. I thought about Nikolas fisting me, and I crowned. It was not easy, but it was going to happen. I bore down to force the baby further along. My sphincter flew open, and the baby popped out like a salmon on a fishing boat. A doctor caught him, and a nurse snipped the umbilical cord. They wrapped our baby in a sterile blanket and rushed him out.

A few hours later, they brought the baby back to us. Nikolas squeezed my hand. The nurse asked, "Do you have a name?"

I looked at Nikolas. "What do you think?"

He smiled, "Colin."

In the days leading up to today, I learned a few things. First, Nelson, the nurse, was part of Dr. Prizziti's plan. Nikolas was not aware, but Dr. Prizziti said that my psychological makeup showed that I would release the most beneficial hormones if I was titillated and frightened at the same time while being stretched out deeper than Nikolas had gone. In private, I met with Nelson, who apologized for scaring me. I told him I would forgive him if he kissed me and fucked me one more time. He wheeled me to our private room and fucked me silly. Without the gag, I was free to kiss him while he violated my worn-out hole. We said our tearful goodbyes.

Nikolas waited patiently while my sigmoid colon was rejoined to the descending colon. My colostomy was removed, and pretty soon, I was pooping like a normal man. The hospital released me and Colin yesterday.

Today, I'm at Nikolas's and my new home in the West Hollywood Hills above the Sunset Strip. My beautiful baby is bouncing on my knee. We're having a small dinner party with Clarissa, Patsy, and a few mutual friends. Sirena sold the Clara Bow house and moved to Mexico, so she wasn't invited.

Colin is a quiet baby. He doesn't cry unless he wants to nurse. The hormones I take ensure I can produce "father's milk" for my little boy. Nikolas confessed that he gets a hard-on watching me nurse. We plan to take care of it later tonight.

Since my pregnancy began, there have been successful pregnancies in Germany, France, England, India and Brazil. Using my rocky road as a map, they thank me for being so brave; it ensured that these miracle babies will be born safely and with proper preparation. The medical science isn't perfect, but they believe that an anal canal birth is more likely to thrive than a surgical extraction, so surprise, surprise, these men will all get fisted by their chosen partners. In Beverly Hills, a clinic has opened. For upwards of $100,000.00, the doctors promise to impregnate men and guarantee the fetus will reach the second trimester. If you think about it, 91 days is the second trimester. Not a big promise.

With Nikolas and his protective PR team, I have only the best interviews. The Nobel committee contacted me and asked me to save a date in the near future. All these miracles can be traced back to a drunken orgy in the Hollywood Hills. Or, if you take a broader view, it can be traced to a sexual friendship between two high school boys in Van Nuys.

THE THIGH BABY

The fable runs, that Semele, Jupiter's mistress, having bound him by an inviolable oath to grant her an unknown request, desired he would embrace her in the same form and manner he used to embrace Juno; and the promise being irrevocable, she was burnt to death with lightning in the performance. The embryo, however, was sewed up, and carried in Jupiter's thigh till the complete time of its birth; but the burden thus rendering the father lame, and causing him pain, the child was thence called Dionysus. - Francis Bacon, Wisdom of the Ancients, Essay XXIV 1597

FOREWORD BY THE AUTHOR

We have only begun to explore the limits of biology. Scientists are unlocking codes hidden in our blood that dictate who we become physically and mentally. As the universe's secrets are revealed, we will likely find a way for men to bear babies. We know there are not enough chromosomes in spermatozoa to yield a complete human being. Still, biologists can extract ova from women, fertilize them, and someday will be able to implant them in vitro, allowing barren women to give birth. It is not impossible that steroidal hormones could create in men an environment capable of housing an embryo. We needn't be Greek Gods to give birth.

Similarly, as these codes are unlocked, we will find the secret that causes some men to be blessed beyond compare, perhaps overly blessed, while others are left with little between their legs. This could be engineered through hormonal therapies or other growth factors to elicit a change from female to male or to make a small man much larger.

This story explores the themes of penis size and male pregnancy. It's also an unapologetic indulgence of the passions of gay sex. It is not for the faint of heart.

Dale Clark was a bully when he was younger. He constantly compared himself to the other boys in the gym shower and came up wanting. His tall, wide stature made his already below-average penis appear tiny. Not surprisingly, he chose to victimize a boy like Jay Benson. Jay was short, skinny, and his dick hung down like a small elephant trunk between his legs. One day, after a particularly violent dodgeball game, Dale cornered Jay in the showers after the other boys left. He held Jay's head to the shower, forcing water up his nose. He punched him until he vomited. Jay was still unaware that he had an enviable prize between his legs. He had no idea what he had done to invoke Dale's wrath. The beatings continued mercilessly until one day, Jay fought back. He punched Dale so hard he started to cry. Blood poured from his nostrils. Jay spat on Dale and told him to fuck off. It was the blossoming of a peculiar friendship. They became good buddies, then something much more than that.

In their senior year, Dale's hormones raged to the point that he could no longer resist his natural urges, which had driven him to torture Jay in the first place. Dale wanted to suck Jay's cock. He wanted it in his ass. He wanted to be a tiny dicked man in subservience to

Jay's almighty cock. Not knowing how to put these words together, he invited Jay to join him in the woods to smoke weed and drink a few Lucky Lagers. Jay had forgiven Dale, but he still had a post-traumatic fear that Dale would turn on him. He was half right.

In the woods, Dale rolled a joint the size of Jay's middle finger, which was considerable. Jay cracked open a couple of brews and tossed the caps on the ground. Dale picked them up to solve the rebus on the inside. The first rebus was a 2000-pound weight, a hatchet, a needle and thread, the letter S, and a coffee mug. He struggled with it. Jay grabbed it and studied it. "It says Ton Axe Sew S Mug."

Dale smiled, "Don't act so smug."

Jay grinned and took a puff from the smoking joint. "What do I have to be smug about?"

Dale shrugged. "If you don't know, you're oblivious."

Jay gestured to the swollen lump of flesh running down his thigh. "You mean this?"

Dale nodded.

Jay scowled. "It's not exactly a great thing to be this big. Do you think a girl would ever want to put this inside her?"

Dale swallowed hard. He looked at the next rebus. "It's a stocking, a microphone, and an eagle or something."

Jay said, "Sock, mike hawk." He burst out laughing. "Suck my cock! I don't believe you; let me see that!"

Dale had made it up. He threw the bottle cap into the woods. "You asked for it."

He pushed Jay off of the log and unbuttoned his jeans. Jay wasn't into guys, but he was desperate to get off, and Dale was more than convenient.

"What are you doing?"

Dale fished in Jay's pants, pulling the half-hard log of flesh out of his pant leg. He put the head, small and pink, into his mouth. The head was pretty small, but the cock was like an ICBM made of spongy, hardening flesh. Dale struggled to fit it in his mouth.

"Ow! Watch the teeth!"

Neither boy had any experience with sex. Dale had jacked off a thousand times thinking about Jay's huge cock, but now that it was finally in his mouth, he worried he'd bit off more than he could chew, especially now that his teeth were scraping Jay's precious cock. He opened his jaws as wide as possible and let the beast go deeper into his mouth.

Jay said, "Shit, Dale, you're good!"

Dale couldn't say anything because, at that moment, he felt Jay's small head enter his throat, blocking the airway. Jay's animal instinct took over. He held Dale by the back of the head and fucked his mouth, each inward thrust reaching a little deeper in his throat. After twenty or thirty thrusts, Dale found his rhythm. He could take in air on the backstroke and loosen his throat muscles to accommodate the thickness. He coughed up phlegm once or twice, making Jay's big boner slippery. Jay encountered no friction as he buried himself down his friend's throat so that his pubic hair tickled his nose.

Dale held Jay's backside, letting the giant cock fill his throat to the point of bursting. His jaws were aching terribly.

"Shit, I'm gonna cum." Jay tried to pull away, but Dale held him firmly in place. "Oh, God! Oh, Jesus Christ! Fuck! I'm right there!" With those words, Jay pumped a warm flood of sperm directly into Dale's stomach. Dale wanted to taste it, but not as badly as he wanted to worship Jay's fat cock.

Jay did a full body shiver. "I ain't queer."

Dale pulled back and licked the last droplets from the tiny piss slit at the end of Jay's fat log. "Me neither, bro. I just dig your cock. It's not a gay thing, it's just us."

Jay nodded. "If you were a girl, I'd fuck you."

"I'm practically a girl. I came in my pants just sucking you off," Dale said.

Jay laughed. "Your little guy was stiff? I didn't even notice."

"Look." Dale pointed to the spreading stain in his jeans. "I think I better take 'em off so they can dry." Dale bent over to untie his sneakers, and Jay caressed his butt cheeks.

"I hear some boys have pussies in their ass," Jay said.

Dale pulled off his jeans. He had so little between his legs he never bothered with underwear. "Yeah, I think I heard about that, too." Dale had been reading gay pulp fiction he found in his dad's bedroom, and he knew all too well what men could do to each other in the butt.

Jay's eyes twinkled. "Look at that tiny thing. I never noticed how small it is."

Dale frowned. He looked down at his pathetic little penis. It was buried in a forest of pubic hair. His eyes teared up.

Jay said, "It's cute. I like it, dude. I wanna see it shoot."

Dale grinned. "Then fuck me in the ass. I bet you I'll shoot so far, I'll hit that tree." He pointed to a tree across the clearing.

Jay said, "You're on!"

Dale read all about butt sex but didn't know how hard it was to get started. He didn't have any Vaseline. He'd read a story where one cowboy just spat on his dick a few times.

Jay spread Dale's cheeks and looked at the tight, virgin hole. "Dude, there's no way you can take me."

"Maybe the tip". Dale pointed to the tapered little head on Jay's otherwise gargantuan cock. "Use some spit."

Then Jay did something Dale couldn't believe. He

buried his nose between Dale's fleshy cheeks and licked the tight hole, spitting and tonguing until it loosened a tiny bit.

Jay stood up, pushing Dale forward onto the log so his ass pointed skyward. He put the tip in. Dale was prepared for pain, but it was fine. Then Jay pushed a little.

Dale felt a searing pain as his anus was forced open a little wider. "Stop!"

Jay waited patiently.

"Okay, go slow and spit on it."

Jay hocked a loogie and let it drop onto his wide cock. He pushed another inch into Dale's tortured hole.

Dale pounded the log, splinters embedding in his fist. He howled.

Jay stopped. "I'm sorry, I don't think you can handle it, man."

Dale hissed over his shoulder. "Fuck me, Jay!"

Jay held Dale's waist and pushed in further. Dale made cattle noises. Jay just kept going until he hit a wall in the back. There was still an inch to go.

Dale read about this. He knew Jay could turn the corner and hit the sweet spot, the second hole. He twisted first one way, then the other. Suddenly, Jay pushed forward all the way.

"Holy shit, did I tear a hole?"

Dale shook his head. "Nah, it's the second hole. It feels good."

"It feels fucking great," Jay said.

Slowly, Jay took a step back, letting his fat cock slide out of Dale's ass. It fell and smacked his leg. "Oops. I went too far."

Dale grabbed his friend's cock and put it right back inside him. This time, there was still too much pain to bear, but it wasn't as bad as the first time.

"Am I hurting you?"

Dale shook his head. It was a lie, but he knew it just

had to feel good at some point, even with Jay's ungodly fat cock splitting him in two. "Nah, man, fuck me."

Jay needed no further encouragement. He swiveled his pelvis like a dog fucking its bitch. Each time he popped through the second hole, Dale moaned.

Jay was done asking if Dale was alright. He grabbed his waist and started fucking at a breakneck speed. His hips were a blur as they pounded Dale's rump over and over. There was a loud clapping sound coming from Dale's ass.

Dale felt the log of flesh sliding in and out. It felt like Jay was owning him. As if Jay was taking control of him, breeding him, punishing him for his past transgressions. His tiny cock was pressed up against the end of the log. The contact with the wood was enough to start him leaking a slow drip.

As if Jay could read his mind, he rotated Dale so that his back was against the log and his little pee-pee pointed skyward. Jay put a hand on it and massaged it like a clitoris. "Your little dick is so fucking hot, dude."

Dale blushed. He'd beat the shit out of Jay for having a big one, never realizing how much Jay liked it small. He put a hand on Jay's, stopping him.

"I'll cum too quick."

Jay concentrated on pushing his cock past the second hole. He fucked furiously, hitting Dale's cheeks so hard with his thighs that they turned red. Dale wrapped his legs around his friend's waist and closed his eyes. He couldn't believe his fantasies were coming true after so many years. He wanted to be the little bitch taking that fat cock up his boy cunt. It made him feel wanted, needed, and so good.

The way Jay looked into his eyes, sweat dripping down his brow, Dale knew he held the real power at that moment. The connection between them grew stronger as they explored each other's eyes, looking to understand the ever-tightening bond that formed between them.

Jay said, "I'm gonna —"

"I know. Me, too."

Jay suddenly stopped, buried to the hilt, and let a massive flood of young-man cum gurgle into Dale's wrecked colon.

Without touching himself, Dale closed his eyes and felt his little cock shoot stream after stream of cum over his head. The fourth spurt landed in his hair, then on his face, then across his t-shirt.

Jay laughed. "Holy fuck, dude, you really hit that tree."

Dale didn't doubt it. Even just whacking his tiny penis in his room had destroyed several wall posters. Jay stayed inside his friend as he helped him sit up. After a minute, Jay was soft, and he fell out of Dale. A gushing waterfall of cum poured out of Dale's destroyed hole.

Jay shook his head. "Yep, that's a pussy." He wiped the grey lips of Dale's stretched-out ass, playing with them. Dale groaned because it felt so good.

Jay said, "Does it really feel good?"

Dale widened his eyes, nodding. "The fucking best."

Jay laughed. "Well, you won't be able to show me."

It was true. Dale's micropenis would never know the inside of Jay's ass. And that was okay with him. He was happy to give and receive so much pleasure in the one-way transaction.

2

ENTER MARLA

Dale and Jay worked at a lube shop in downtown Springfield that summer after senior year. They fucked and sucked every chance they got. Then Marla came along and ruined everything. Dale's sister, Marla Clark, was pretty, funny, sweet, and totally in love with Jay. It was mutual. Jay stopped fucking Dale on the nights when he dated Marla. He didn't know that Dale was in love with him. He'd talk about how she couldn't suck him, but her pussy was so loose he went in without any spit at all. Dale listened, pretending to be fascinated, but inside, he was seething. He didn't want to think about his lucky sister and her magic pussy.

Dale and Marla's folks paid for a big apartment so she and Jay could live together. Jay wanted Dale to suck him off since Marla was sorely lacking in that department, so he suggested he move into a spare room where they were just storing boxes.

On mornings when they were both off work, and Marla was keeping books at the brick factory, Jay would sit on the couch and pull out his cock. Dale would kneel between his legs and swallow the whole thing down to the base. This was one of those mornings.

"Oh fuck, Dale, you're so good at that."

"Mnph!" Dale took tiny breaths and saved up enough air to let out a sound every so often.

They had learned to put a towel on the couch that draped down to the floor. This caught most of Dale's cum. Marla did the laundry and asked about it more than once, but she never suspected what it really meant. "It's her own fucking fault," Dale thought, "She just isn't willing to give head like she should."

Jay stopped fucking Dale in the ass now that he had pussy every night. Dale felt empty inside without Jay's cock up there. He loved his sister despite all she stood for. She created a wedge between friends, and it got a little wider that morning.

Jay and Dale timed it so they both came at the same time. Dale imagined he was the owner of the big powerful cock pumping its seed into his throat. He wondered if Jay pretended to be him. Probably not.

Jay's chest heaved as he shot the last of his load down Dale's throat. The phone rang. Jay waited until he caught his breath, answering on the sixth ring.

Dale could only hear one side of the conversation. "Hello?... What's up, sweetie?... I was taking a dump; that's why I'm out of breath. Oh...oh...that's good, right?"

Dale smacked Jay's bare leg to get his attention. He mouthed, "What?"

Jay shook his head. "No, babe, that's the best news ever. I mean it...Okay...I love you."

Jay smiled at Dale. "Dude, I'm gonna be a dad!"

3

A WILD RIDE

Dale's only consolation as he watched his childhood crush prepare for the damnation of fatherhood was that Marla didn't want to have sex anymore. Her pussy was closed for business, so Jay started fucking Dale again. It was like getting back on a bicycle. It hurt so bad he limped the first day. But by the second time, he opened wide and spread his man pussy to take the whole thing like a girl.

It was six months into Marla's pregnancy, and Dale was giving Jay the full service. He soaked Jay's cock with his throat juices, then sat down easily on his cock, landing in his lap and then riding him like a cowgirl. Dale stared at Jay's thick lips and sleepy eyes. He wanted to kiss him so badly. Jay sensed it and pulled back, breaking the bond that was forming.

He rotated Dale so he was facing away in the reverse of the cowgirl position. He lifted Dale's butt an inch or two and fucked upwards hard and fast a hundred times a minute. Dale loved every second of it.

He couldn't hold in his joy. "Oh, fuck! Oh, fuck, Jay!"

"You like it when I fuck your man pussy, don't you?"

Dale nodded. "Make me cum like a girl."

Jay was good at it. He knew just where to press and bend to make Dale drip, then shoot. The cum went so far off the sofa it landed in a wastebasket near the kitchen. Then, it stained the rug. Dale had more than one load inside, so Jay kept fucking it out of him. The second time Dale came, Jay closed his eyes and roared. "Fuck! Oh, Fuck! Take it!"

Dale closed his eyes, shouting over him. "Fill me up with your baby batter, Daddy!" And Jay did just that. Neither heard the door open.

Marla stood with her hands on one hip, her purse in the other. Her baby bump was obscene. The child must be ten pounds. She tapped a shoe angrily.

"What the fuck is this?"

Jay pushed Dale to the ground. "You fucking queer!"

As Jay's cum leaked onto the carpet, Marla said, "You ain't fooling me, Jay. You and Dale have been fucking for years. You think I didn't know?"

"Nah, he just blows me. He sat on my dick just now cause he's a fucking queer. That's all."

"Save it!"

Jay stood up, not bothering to hide his colossal, soft, dripping cock. He put an arm on Marla's shoulder. "You know I need it every day. Look at it." He pointed to his cock. "When it's this big, you gotta feed it pussy all the time. I fuck Dale out of respect for you and the baby."

It was ridiculous, and Dale knew it. He was furious, ashamed, and depressed. He knew why Jay was lying, but knowing didn't make it hurt any less.

Jay offered to take them to the Golden Dragon to talk it out in a private booth over pot stickers and Kung Pao Chicken. Marla reluctantly agreed. Dale didn't want to be shut out of the conversation, so he tagged along.

The restaurant served Chinese Beer, which seemed much more potent than American Beer. The tension at the table led to a lot of beer between the two men. Marla sipped her Shirley Temple, rolling her eyes.

"Honey, me and Dale are like fuck buddies, but you got nothing to worry about. I don't love him. I love you."

Marla looked at Dale. "Is that true?"

Dale nodded, taking a big swig from the beer bottle, fighting back tears.

Marla narrowed her eyes. "You love him, though, don't you."

Dale was too drunk to protest. "Yeah, I fucking love him. I've loved him since seventh grade."

Jay turned deep red. "You what? What kind of fucking queer are you?"

Dale just took another big swig of Tsing Tao and looked away.

Marla put a hand on Dale's arm. "Don't you see, Dale, you're different than Jay. You could go to the city and find other guys like you. I hear there's lots of them."

Dale stared her down, a drunken haze blocking his view. "I ain't queer. I'm in love with Jay. He's the only person I love in the whole goddamn world, and he's in love with you."

Jay, nearly as drunk as Dale, took a swing at his fuck buddy. Dale caught his fist mid-air and crushed it with his giant hands. If the waiter hadn't shown up with the check, they would have gotten into a full brawl.

At the car, Marla demanded to drive. Jay was so angry and drunk that he just pushed her. "No! I'm the man. I drive, woman."

Marla smacked Jay, who grabbed her by both wrists and shook her. "Lissen, Marla, I'm driv-driving." Dale climbed in the back seat of the Nash Rambler, and Marla rolled her eyes before sitting in the front passenger seat.

Jay tore out of the parking lot at high speed. He roared down Highway 45, pedal to the metal.

"Slow down, Jay!" Marla was terrified. Dale didn't care. He wanted to die.

Jay kept looking at Dale in the rearview mirror. The loathing on his face was unbearable. Dale lay down and napped. He woke up in the hospital.

❧ 4 ☙

THE THIGH

The first thing Dale heard was monitors beeping. As the room slowly came into view, he became aware of a searing pain in his right thigh. Next was an aching tightness between his neck and right shoulder. He couldn't see under the blanket, but he thought maybe he'd broken his leg, except it felt much stranger than that. He turned his head to the right, wincing, to see a bandage holding his collarbone in place. A nurse saw him and ran to get the doctor.

The doctor came in, a dire expression on his face. "I'm sorry, son, your wife didn't make it."

"I don't have a wife."

There was a commotion between the doctor and the nurse. "But you have the same last name."

"She's my sister."

There were more murmurs, and the doctor said, "I'm so sorry your sister died of smoke inhalation yesterday."

Dale went numb. In a monotone, he asked, "How's Jay?"

The doctor stepped aside, revealing a perfectly intact Jay wearing a worried expression. He had some bruising, and both eyes were black, but otherwise, he seemed fine.

"Hey buddy, I'm sorry." Jay burst into tears. Dale had no sympathy for the bastard. It made him sick to watch the man he loved crying over his sister, whom he had killed with his drunken foolishness.

The nurse whispered in the doctor's ear. He looked cross when he said, "I'm getting to that. Take five." The nurse shrugged and left the room.

Dale could sense something wasn't quite right. "Doc, am I gonna die or something?"

Jay and the doctor turned to one another. Jay wiped the tears from his eyes. "I'm sorry, Dale. I was unconscious."

Dale sat up, wincing as his right thigh and collarbone shot arrows of pain up his spine. "What the fuck is going on?"

The doctor took out a needle and plugged it into the saline drip. "Calm down, son. This is just a sedative. Wait a minute."

In about fifteen seconds, nothing mattered. Dale couldn't remember a day in his life when he felt this calm. The doctor could have told him anything, and it would have just rolled off him like water off a duck's back.

"You're going to be fine. You just broke your collarbone. Your sister didn't survive, but her baby did. It was still too premature. We did a radical procedure."

The doctor pulled back the blanket, revealing Dale's swollen thigh. There was an incision and black sutures running across the top.

Dale smiled. "What's that?" He didn't care, but it seemed fitting to ask.

"It's called a Dionysian section."

Jay said, "Yeah, it's uh, it's my baby. Marla's baby."

Dale touched the sutures and winced. "I don't understand."

The doctor removed his stethoscope and put the

ends in Dale's ear, holding the diaphragm to his femoral artery. "What do you hear?"

Dale listened. "I hear my heartbeat."

The doctor nodded and moved the diaphragm a few inches from the artery. "What do you hear now?"

Dale's eyes widened. "I hear two heartbeats. Mine, and a fast one."

"That's your sister's baby. We implanted it in your thigh."

Dale should have freaked out, but the sedative was growing in strength. His eyes fluttered, and he fell asleep.

A NURSE'S COMFORT

Dale awoke sobbing. In an instant, Jay had changed every aspect of his life. His sister Marla was gone. He may have hated her for stealing the love of his life, but she was still his blood. Under the hatred ran a cool river of unconditional love, but right now, it was just a trickle, an arroyo.

Jay had rejected him completely. He'd called him a faggot and pushed him away. Dale knew he deserved it for all the times he'd made Jay's life miserable through torture, violence, extortion, and other cruel bullying tactics. That didn't make the rejection hurt any less.

He was alone in the hospital room, and the gnawing ache in his stomach, he realized, wasn't just sadness over the rejection. He was ravenous. He pushed the call button. A handsome male nurse came in.

"Hey, what's up?"

"Uh, hi. I'm like super hungry."

The nurse gave a wide grin. "That's great. It means you're alive, my friend. I'll be right back."

Dale stared in fascination as the nurse turned to leave the room. His body touched the uniform in more places than he would have expected. His nurse was a bodybuilder, for sure. The rock-solid ass wiggled as he walked away.

In a few moments, he returned, carrying a tray of bland hospital food. "I'm Carlos, your night nurse." He put the tray in front of Dale, who struggled to feed himself with his left hand. "Hey, Dale, let me help you with that."

As Carlos cut the breaded chicken breast, his biceps pulsed and bulged. Dale couldn't help himself. He put his hand partway around Carlos's muscle.

"Yeah, I work out. It's big, don't you think?"

Dale nodded. "You're fucking stacked, bro."

Carlos took Dale's hand and put it on his pectoral muscles. "Do you feel that?" Dale smiled. Carlos flexed his chest muscles one at a time, causing his shirt to lift slightly. Carlos moved his hand down to his belly. Even through the cotton shirt, the abdominal muscles were hard as a rock and rippled like a carton of eggs.

"In bodybuilding, we call that an eight-pack."

Dale looked below the waist and gasped. Something was lurking in Carlos's pants, straining against the fabric.

Carlos grinned. "And I call that my nine-pack." Dale withdrew his hand, but Carlos grabbed his wrist and placed it on his crotch. It was huge. Dale wasn't too shabby. He had a flat stomach and broad shoulders. But he wasn't ripped, and, of course, his little girl dick was shamefully small compared to the chunk of meat Carlos carried around.

"Eat up, buddy." Carlos resumed feeding Dale, his hard-on throbbing between his pants. "Between you and me, I changed your bedpan a few times while you were out. You have a sweet little ass." He winked.

Dale blushed. "I-I'm not a queer if that's what you're thinking."

Carlos laughed. "With that little dick, you better consider it. You ain't gonna get no girl pregnant with that. But you could make a man like me feel pretty good. " He took away the tray. "You ain't eaten in 48 hours. You're clean down there. I wiped you myself. But I gotta change your bedpan anyway."

Carlos closed the curtain, then carefully rolled Dale to one side, so he rested on his left shoulder. Carlos whistled. "You sure you ain't queer?"

Dale couldn't shrug. "No, but I like to get fucked."

Carlos produced a tube of KY Jelly from his pants pocket. He pressed it against Dale's hole and squeezed. The jelly, warmed in Carlos's pocket, swept through Dale's loose crevice and moistened his rectum.

Carlos stuck a finger in Dale's asshole, twisting it around before adding a second, then a third.

"Damn, you are loose, bro. I love a loose ass. It takes forever to get this inside my girlfriend."

Dale said, "Yeah, I got a friend who's really thick."

Carlos whistled. He reached into his pants and pulled out a half-hard cock to rival Jay's. The head was pink, poking through the foreskin, much larger than Jay's. The shaft was longer and dark brown. "It takes a minute to get hard." He touched Dale's already rock-hard, dripping nipple of a dick. "Not much down there, right?"

Dale scowled. "I didn't choose to be this way."

"You're beautiful, man. I love your ass, your little dick, your big body. If you lifted, you could be as big as me," Carlos said. "Not your dick, obviously."

Carlos jerked his cock with KY jelly until it had swollen to its full size. It wasn't nearly as thick as Jay's but far thicker than most. And he was longer than Jay by a good two inches. Carlos pressed until his head slipped past Dale's loose anus.

"Sí, papi." Carlos nibbled on Dale's ear. He held his cock at the base to help guide it to the end of Dale's rectum, then twisted and pushed past the second hole. Dale had felt Jay's little head enter that hole hundreds of times, but he'd never felt anything like Carlos. His long cock pushed several inches into the sigmoid colon.

Dale grunted, shocked at how good it felt to be filled but not stretched to the point of pain.

Carlos moved his tongue to Dale's neck, licking and sucking on it. Dale had never been kissed. When Carlos turned his head and pressed their lips together, Dale nearly cried. Why couldn't Jay be this passionate? They said nothing as Carlos moved in and out of the second hole, mashing their lips and tongues together.

Carlos held Dale's waist and increased the strokes like a steam engine leaving the station. Each time he popped through the second hole, Dale quivered.

"You like that, don't you papi?"

Dale nodded vigorously.

Carlos said, "It feels good, don't it?"

In response, Dale moaned softly.

Carlos put a hand over his mouth. "Don't make too much noise, bro."

Then Carlos reached bunny-fucking speed. The sound of his cock smashing through the second hole and his thighs pounding into Dale's ass made a clapping sound. Dale rolled his eyes up into his head, overcome with pleasure.

Carlos kept his hand over Dale's mouth. It smelled like sterile KY jelly and onions. It was a strange combination but nearly put Dale over the edge. He couldn't talk, so he made a very quiet whine of ecstasy.

Carlos whispered in his ear. "I gotta come in your ass. I don't want to clean up my mess."

Thinking about Carlos shooting his load in his ass made Dale cum. He hadn't realized Carlos put a bed pan next to his dick; it made a loud metallic 'ding' each time Dale shot a load.

"Damn, papi, you cum hard. Oh, fuck, that little dick is so damn hot. Oh shit. Ay, Dios! I'm coming!"

Carlos threw his head back, revealing his perfect abs. He pressed all the way into Dale's colon, filling it with his spicy Latin cum.

As soon as Carlos finished, he pulled his stiff cock out, making Dale jump as it popped out of his hole.

"Clean it." He pressed his drippy cock into Dale's mouth and down his throat. "That's it. Nice and clean."

While Dale was spit-shining Carlos's softening cock, the nurse wiped Dale's ass with a little towel.

"You didn't even bleed. I never seen a guy that didn't bleed a little after I fucked him."

Carlos withdrew his cock; it hit his leg with a loud smack. Carlos pulled up his scrubs and tightened the drawstring.

"I gotta go. The lady in 3B needs my dick bad."

Dale said, "Will you come back?"

Carlos frowned. "I thought you said you ain't no fag. I don't do repeats. Not with dudes."

Dale, starved for the affection Carlos had shown, felt a hollow space open in his heart. He said, "Yeah. I just liked your dick in my ass. I ain't a fag. It felt good. I thought you might want to do it again."

Carlos shook his head. "Nope." He slid the bedpan under Dale's ass and left the room. Dale cried himself to sleep, dreaming of Jay kissing him like Carlos Had.

❦ 6 ❦

A HUG AND A KISS

The following day, the doctor said Dale was ready to leave. The morning nurse removed his bedpan, frowning at the contents, but she said nothing. Dale had a feeling that Carlos did this a lot, and it wasn't the first time she'd seen something suspicious in there.

An orderly helped Dale into a wheelchair. He and the doctor rolled him out to the lobby, where Jay was waiting with crossed arms.

The doctor showed Dale and Jay two prescription bottles.

"This one is progesterone. Dale needs to take this three times a day. This one is Tylenol III with Codeine. You only take that if the pain is awful. Otherwise, take regular Tylenol.

In his sweatpants, Dale's right leg looked bizarre. It was so fat in his upper thigh that it looked like he was as stacked as Carlos, but only just in his right thigh.

Jay rolled Dale out to the parking lot. When he went over a speed bump, Dale farted cum. His sweatpants were surely stained now. Jay wouldn't notice or care. He didn't care about Dale at all. Or so he thought.

Jay transferred Dale to the rental car. He could stand on his left leg, but his right leg was still useless.

Jay folded up the wheelchair and sat down next to Jay. He put the keys in the ignition but didn't start the car. He just stared at the steering wheel.

Dale asked, "Are you okay?"

Jay smiled. "I should be asking you, not the other way around. I'm fine; I just have a lot on my mind."

Dale felt the fetus kick. It stretched the sutures and made him wince. "I'm fine, Jay. Really."

Jay perked up. "You mean you don't mind carrying my baby?"

Dale felt a flood of emotion hearing those words. It might have just been the hormones, but he was desperate to feel love from Jay, and he just realized they were forever linked by this life growing in him. It was crumbs, but he would take whatever Jay could give him.

Dale couldn't hold back the tears. He tried to talk, but the words came in heaving sobs. "I just want to make you happy."

Then Jay did something he'd never done before. He hugged Dale and kissed his cheek.

"I am happy. My best friend is alive." He started the car, and they drove home.

Dale put one arm around Jay's shoulder and hopped up the steps to the apartment. He flopped down on the sofa while Jay retrieved the meds and wheelchair.

"Should I sleep on the couch?"

"Nah, man," Jay said, "You should probably sleep with me in case you need to pee in the middle of the night or whatever."

Jay stood in front of Dale, hands on his hips. It was a familiar stance—the same old song and dance. Dale unbuttoned Jay's jeans and pulled them to his ankles. Jay was already hard, and his cock smacked Dale's Chin. Dale pretended that Jay's cock was his lips, and when he inhaled it, he used his tongue like he had done with Carlos.

"Oh shit, Dale, that feels good."

"Mmm hmm." It felt great. He couldn't kiss Jay, but he could suck his cock with love. He pulled Jay close, forcing the unbelievably long, thick cock down his throat. He didn't care how much it hurt when it pushed past his voice box. He just sucked lovingly, like a kiss deep in his throat.

The electricity between the two was something new. Dale looked up at Jay, expecting him to have his eyes closed, imagining it was some girl, but Jay was looking back, smiling. Their eyes locked, but Jay just stared instead of looking away; a single tear formed in the corner of his eye.

"Nobody can suck my cock but you, Dale. You're amazing."

Now it was Dale's turn to cry, but the tears wouldn't stop. The damn hormones were fucking with his emotions.

"Hey, hey, come here." Jay pulled out, leaving Dale gasping for air. Jay kissed his forehead. "You don't have to suck my dick."

Dale shook his head. "No, those tears were just the pills. Keep going."

Jay was losing his hard-on. Dale put it back in his mouth and sucked until it swelled up again.

Jay said, "I wish we could fuck."

Dale took the massive cock out of his mouth and jerked it with his hands. "Why can't we?"

Jay said, "I don't know, I mean, the doctor didn't say we could."

Dale knew they could. Carlos had shown him how. But he couldn't tell Jay that.

"I mean, he didn't say we couldn't, right?" Dale looked hungrily at Jay's throbbing dick. "I could lie on my left side like this."

Dale pulled down his sweats, exposing his slippery hole.

"Why is your ass wet?"

Dale thought fast. "It's the hormones. The doctor told me it might happen." It was old cum and KY Jelly, but Jay didn't know that.

"Will it hurt the baby?"

Dale wasn't a doctor, but Carlos would never have fucked him if it wasn't safe. He said, "No. Not if you do it like you're making love, not just fucking."

Jay said, "What, like I was a faggot?" His cock started to droop.

"No, I mean like I was Marla. You know, gentle."

Dale had walked in more than once on them fucking. He knew, from her screams, that Jay would always take it slower and gentler with her. Like he loved her and wanted more than just to get off inside her. Dale wanted to be that for Jay.

Dale licked the tip of Jay's cock, kissing it, pretending they were kissing, and it got hard again. "Really, Jay, I know how hard it must be having to jack off alone. Just fuck me. You know it feels better."

Jay didn't need any further persuading. He got on one knee and pushed his cock into Dale's slippery hole. It had to be the hormones, but Dale felt less pain than usual. As Jay plugged his hole, pushing past the second one, Dale relaxed, letting him in further than ever before.

"Oh shit, Dale, that feels good."

"Fuck me," Dale said.

And Jay did, but not the rough, angry sex. He made love to Dale. Instead of just fucking until he dumped his load, Jay paused periodically to ask Dale if it felt good.

"It feels great. Just like that, Jay. Just like that. Right there."

Jay didn't fuck for his pleasure alone. He was making sure Dale felt good, too. And he did. He started dripping a salty trail of pre-cum onto the couch. They had forgotten a towel, It was going to stain, but Dale didn't give a fuck.

Jay stretched Dale like a sausage casing with each slow, deliberate thrust. He pushed into the colon, holding it there a second or two before pulling back. When Jay put a hand on Dale's chest to hold him closer, he brushed a nipple. Dale shot his first load. It flew across the room. His shirt was wet. There was milk coming out of his nipples. When Jay saw that, his eyes bugged out.

"Oh fuck that's hot." He leaned over, lifted Dale's shirt, and sucked on his nipple. It was the most intimate moment they had ever shared. Dale came again and again, like a woman, until he thought his balls would run dry. Jay's slow, deliberate strokes stopped as he nursed from Dale's milky tits. He was buried to his pubes, vibrating from the electromagnetic bond they had formed. He shot his load deep inside Dale.

Jay lifted his head, staring Dale in the eyes. "What is this? Why do I feel like this?"

Dale put a finger on Jay's chin and tugged him close. He planted his lips on Jay's.

They kissed like he had seen Jay do with Marla so many times. Jay didn't pull away. He leaned into it. With Jay still hard inside him, Dale felt a churning in his balls. He came again. Jay started his gentle strokes again, kissing Dale passionately. It didn't take long until Jay shot a second load. They collapsed, exhausted. When Jay got soft, Dale's guts kicked him out. His soft, drippy cock landed on the sofa, followed by a tidal wave of cum. They continued to kiss until Dale's stomach growled.

"I'll make you breakfast." Jay got up and put some bacon in the pan. Dale feared losing whatever that had been, but he dared not say anything. Three words could turn Jay cold as ice. He couldn't say, "I love you."

7

HOUSE CALLS

That night, Jay carried Dale in his arms to the bed he'd never slept in before. The pillows felt softer than he'd imagined. The mattress was no better than his own, but it felt like the baby bear's bed in Goldilocks for some reason. As any man would recognize, the two men shared a strange coldness after making love. Jay slept on one side, a foot away from Dale. But in the middle of the night, Jay rolled over and put his arm around Dale, waking him. Dale ran his fingers through Jay's. It was ironic how huge Dale's hands were compared to Jay's, yet in the dick department, Jay was a whale to Dale's minnow. The relationship between the two body parts was a myth.

When Dale woke the following day, Jay was already at work. When Dale got himself out of bed into his wheelchair, he found a bowl of oatmeal covered in foil waiting for him on the kitchen table.

Jay worked at the lube shop during the day and fucked Dale at night. The tenderness they had known that first night vanished. Jay went back to his mechanical, rough fucking. Dale knew it would happen. The love between them wasn't real. Even when Jay nursed from Dale's tits, he did it like a kid eating a candy bar, not a lover sharing an intimate moment. The lube shop owner knew Jay's strange situation, and that he was strapped for cash, so he promoted him to manager, which meant lots more money but more extended hours. Dale was alone for hours.

The state sent a visiting nurse daily to change his bandages and check his levels. It was rarely the same nurse twice. Some of the nurses that came were old battle axes, and some were pretty young girls. When a male nurse finally showed up, Dale was so desperate for tenderness that he practically threw himself at the man, who was plain, average, and bland. The man didn't respond to Dale's advances. Only Jay paid him any attention, even though it was with the cold indifference he'd known since that first afternoon they fucked.

The baby grew quickly in his leg. His skin stretched like a woman's belly, tight as a drum. The doctor said they needed to wait the full nine months to be sure the baby had no other risks at birth. The sutures came out in the seventh month because the skin had healed.

One day, Carlos walked through the door. He gave a mischievous grin when Dale realized who it was.

"What are you doing here? I thought you worked at the hospital?"

"Yeah, well, I got caught. They didn't exactly fire me, but I had to switch to this. When I saw your sweet ass on the schedule, I put my name in the hat."

Dale scoffed. "I thought you said you don't do repeats."

Carlos shrugged. "I do with women. You're half-woman now."

Dale's shirt got wet as his nipples leaked milk. It was an involuntary response. He'd been craving warmth, and Carlos was a spicy hot lover. Carlos saw the spreading stain.

"Is that...?"

Dale nodded.

Carlos rushed over and lifted Dale's shirt, sucking

on his tits like a starving baby. "Oh fuck, man. This shit makes my dick so hard." He kept sucking, his cock swelling in his khakis. Dale touched the swelling lump that ran down Carlos's leg. It was harder than oak.

The nurse pulled down Dale's sweatpants, revealing the baby lump. He stopped sucking and shook his head. "Dude, your dick is bigger."

Dale laughed. That was impossible. But he looked down, and sure enough, his hard dick was at least two inches now. It had been no more than an inch a few weeks before.

Carlos said, "I don't give a shit. It's still a pathetic little dick. Just the way I like them."

Carlos surveyed Dale's body. "Yeah, your hips are wider, and you got bitch tits."

Carlos pulled off his rugby shirt, revealing his rippling upper body for the first time. Dale's little dick throbbed. The contours of Carlos's body were unreal. He was like an inverted pyramid. Love lines ran from his waist across his lower abdomen, disappearing in his tight khakis. Dale had felt but had never seen an eight-pack before. It made Michelangelo's David look pudgy by comparison. His shoulders were as big around as grapefruits. His nipples were two saucers in a sea of tight muscle. His handsome face sat atop a sinewy brown neck. He leaned forward, putting that thick neck against Dale's mouth.

"Go ahead, give me a hickey." Dale nursed on the flesh, tasting the testosterone that fueled Carlos's incredible muscle growth.

A dark bruise appeared on the nurse's neck. Carlos put his mouth on Dale's neck, ready to return the favor.

"Don't leave a mark, please. My roommate won't like it."

Carlos laughed. "Okay, papi. I won't."

He turned around and unzipped his khakis, stepping out of them. He revealed Herculean thighs, bigger around than Dale's pregnant leg. His calves were like giant arrowheads of flesh, pointing upwards toward his perfect ass. His long, fat, uncut brown cock swung from thigh to thigh, plainly visible from behind. He turned around, revealing his full frontal splendor.

Dale used his good arm to reach out and lift the apple-sized head to his mouth. Unlike Jay, Carlos had a mushroom head that flared. It made a slurping sound as it moved in and out of his mouth, then later, as it slipped past his tonsils. Carlos was huge by any standards, but his cock was still thinner than Jay's. It was such a relief to suck a cock that didn't hurt his jaw. When Carlos was good and hard, he took out a tube of KY. He slicked up his cock and wiped the leftovers around Dale's loose hole.

"Damn, Papi, in the daylight, that ass looks just like a pussy. Your roommate must be a fucking donkey."

Dale nodded. "More like an elephant."

Carlos slipped in quickly. Jay had stretched Dale permanently; his anal cavity was a superhighway for cock. Carlos held Dale's cock to steady him and pressed his way in deeper.

Dale moaned loudly. Carlos didn't clap a hand over his mouth this time. He was free to bellow and wail as Carlos pushed past the second hole over and over again. Dale felt so different down there. His tiny penis was bigger. Carlos's fingers fondled more flesh than before. It was odd, wonderful, and a huge turn-on. He churned out a clear river of pre-cum onto the couch.

There was a knock on the door. "Package!"

Carlos pulled out so fast that Dale's ass gave out a floppy fart. Carlos sauntered over to the door and opened it a little.

"Hey, hey. Come on in!"

A huge black bodybuilder clapped a high five with Carlos and strolled in.

"This is my homey Leroy."

The new arrival turned to Carlos. "Man, we went over this. I don't go by Leroy. I'm LT."

"Right, LT. Come meet Dale."

Dale was flummoxed. A stranger just waltzes in while he's bare-ass naked, lubed up, and in the middle of a passionate moment with Carlos.

"Uh, hi. Nice to meet you."

LT didn't waste time shaking hands. He pulled his double-knit polyester pants down, revealing a monstrously fat cock. It was so black it was purple.

Carlos said, "I got him warmed up for you."

LT tugged at his cock, forcing blood into the chambers. It was soft and huge. It didn't grow much as it hardened, and it never got completely hard.

LT grabbed Dale's head, stuffing his cock in his mouth. "Why don't you help, son?"

Dale was surprised by the strange new taste. Carlos tasted of onions; LT tasted of cocoa butter. The spongy flesh filled his mouth and banged into his tonsils. It was soft enough to slide past with gentle pressure. Dale gagged a little, not used to the hard/soft cock that kept moving down like a marshmallow through a keyhole.

Carlos watched. "Damn, dude. He's gonna take the whole thing!"

LT held Dale's ears and pushed until his curly pubic hair touched his upper lip.

"You were right. This boy can suck dick."

Carlos was rock hard watching his friend impale Dale's face.

Dale was shocked that Carlos had just offered him up like a plate of crackers and cheese. He had no say in this. But he was loving it, so he didn't protest.

"I'ma fuck that ass. I hear it's loose. I love loose ass."

Dale nodded as LT pulled out his semi-hard cock, so heavy it swung between his legs repeatedly like a flesh pendulum.

LT inspected Dale's loose ass. "You stretch it for me like that? You ain't that big."

Carlos shook his head. "His boyfriend is probably even thicker than you. He stretches him out every night."

Dale didn't like being discussed in the third person. It made him feel like a hostage. And Jay wasn't his boyfriend. He was the father of his child. His baby's daddy.

LT jerked his cock a few times to wake it up. He pushed into Dale's loose crevice. "Oh fuck that's sweeter than pussy."

LT rutted like a sex-crazed dog. He pummeled Dale's insides, bruising a kidney. The dick was soft enough to turn the corner, but the pressure was intense. The spongy flesh hardened a little with each stroke until soon it felt like LT had rammed a big black sword up his ass. Dale whimpered.

LT smacked him. "Shut up, bitch!"

Dale was rock-hard, and the smack made him leak a load of pre-cum. It was shameful to be turned on so much by this hulking black man mistreating him. He wanted LT to smack him again.

"Hit me."

LT smacked Dale again, raising a red welt on his cheek. "You like it, white boy? You like that huge fucking dick in your shitter?"

Dale nodded.

"Come here, Carlos. The boy needs a double-dicking."

Dale said, "Uh, what's that?"

Carlos didn't answer. He just stuck his dick in beside LT and stretched Dale wider than ever. The pain was intoxicating. His eyes disappeared behind his forehead. Drool came out of his gaping mouth. He couldn't take another second, yet he wanted it to last forever.

It didn't take Carlos long to get fully hard. Dale was

8

LIES AND SEX

D ale couldn't shrug because of his bad shoulder. He said, "I used to bully them in elementary school. The Hispanic dude Carlos was my nurse. He wanted revenge, so he brought that black dude, and they raped me."

It was the best lie he could come up with. Jay changed his demeanor. He rushed over to Dale's side. "Did they hurt you?"

Dale nodded.

Jay inspected Dale's gaping hole. "Shit, you're all stretched out. It looks like a pink slug coming out of your ass."

Dale reached down with his good hand and touched the prolapsed anus. He pushed on it, and it snapped back inside him. It hurt.

Jay kissed Dale on the forehead. "I'm glad you're okay. Is there anything I can do to make you feel better?"

Dale suppressed a smile. "You could fuck me. Maybe kiss me."

Jay laughed. "I don't think anyone should fuck you now. You got turned inside out!"

Dale whined. "Please. It needs someone to push it back in."

Jay sighed. "Let me see you push it out again."

Dale pushed like he was taking a shit. The inside of his ass came rolling out of his loose hole.

Jay shivered. "I don't know why that's so fucking hot, but it is."

Dale pushed it back inside. "I need you to push it all the way up inside me.

Jay was already rock-hard. He pulled off his greasy coveralls. His hard cock was trapped down one leg. When it broke free, it flew upwards, hitting the middle of his chest before bobbing up and down in front of him.

"Do you need any lube?"

Dale shook his head. He was a greased pig inside. Jay put the small head against the pink lips of the sea slug. As his fat cock pushed forward, it stretched the wrinkled pink flesh until it was tucked back in place. He kept going, easily reaching the second hole. He pumped his hips a few times to make sure the mess was going to stay inside. It held firm. Then he humped and rutted like a jackrabbit, pummeling Dale's second hole and stretching his rectum. In moments, Jay shot his load. He waited inside to soften so he could pull out gently. The pink sea slug stayed inside.

He looked down at Dale's cock. "Did that get bigger?"

Dale nodded. "I think it's the baby or the hormones."

Jay said, "Probably both."

He picked Dale up off the couch and brought him to the kitchen table. "I bought us some steaks if you're hungry."

Dale nodded, exhausted. The kitchen chair on his ass felt uncomfortable but not as bad as the swelling baby in his thigh. While Jay cooked the steaks, they spoke about their strange situation.

"Do you want me around once the baby is born?" Dale asked.

Jay frowned. "What do you mean? It's your baby, too, right?"

Dale hadn't thought of it like that. He figured he was just a vessel to carry the kid, nothing more. "You want me around, then?"

Jay snorted. "Of course I do, stupid. I love you."

The words hung in the air like the smoke coming from the searing steaks. Dale saw Jay backpedaling in his mind. He waited for the hurtful words to come next. But they didn't.

"You mean it?"

Jay nodded. "I do, bro. I love you. I guess I'm a fucking queer."

Dale said, "Me, too. I mean, I love you. And I'm a fucking queer."

They laughed. Jay put the steaks on the plate and tossed a salad while they rested. They ate together in silence. Dale stole glances at Jay, waiting for him to deny his love. The denial never came.

After dinner, Jay carried Dale to the couch. They watched professional wrestling. Dale liked the big guys in their tight satin shorts. One wrestler, Snake Eyes, had a monster cock that he proudly displayed.

Dale said, "Shit, he's got a huge one."

Jay growled. "Why are you looking?" His jealousy was sweeter than a tin roof sundae. Dale sighed.

"You got nothing to worry about, Jay. You got the best cock in the world."

Jay puffed up with pride. "Say that again."

"You got the best cock in the world. It's fucking huge, and it feels so good inside me."

Jay's jeans began to strain. The lump in his leg swelled. Dale unbuttoned the fly, but Jay had to lift his butt to pull down the pants, freeing the monster.

While Jay watched wrestling, Dale sucked Jay's dick

like it would buy him dinner. He pushed it deep into his throat, holding his breath for minutes as he stroked it by bobbing up and down. The cock tasted like his ass, and he tasted a little of LT and Carlos, too. Their cum must have coated Jay's cock when he fucked Dale earlier.

"Mmm. Dale, you are a cocksucking champ. You should win an award."

Dale couldn't answer. Each time, he waited until he turned blue to pull back and catch his breath. Two deep breaths and he was back down on Jay, sniffing his pubes.

Jay caressed Dale's hair, gently pushing him down a few moments after he came up for air. This lasted for ten minutes until, at last, Dale felt a salty trickle in his throat that signaled Jay was close.

"Shit, dude, I'm gonna cum."

Dale nodded. Jay held his head and fucked upwards off the couch. Dale coughed while his roommate/lover skull-fucked his mouth.

"Oh, shit, yeah!" Jay plunged in as deep as he'd ever gone, tube-feeding Dale a slippery white dessert of cum.

Dale trembled with orgasm, then felt his little dick spit into Jay's hand. Jay licked it up. "You got so many girl hormones, that shit tastes like pussy juice."

Dale smiled. He'd pleased his man, and it felt good.

9

CHANGES

Jay took the day off to take Dale to the hospital for a checkup. The doctor listened to his leg with a stethoscope, tutting and nodding.

"It's good. We're in new territory. Any sharp pains?"

Dale shook his head. "Only when I move my leg too quick or whatever."

The doctor nodded approvingly. "You're an ideal host. You share plenty of genes with your sister and have the same blood type. We couldn't have asked for a better surrogate." He changed his tone. "Have you noticed any unusual changes in your body?"

Dale laughed. "What hasn't changed? My tits give milk; my dick grew bigger; I feel the baby kicking constantly."

The doctor raised his glasses. "Are you telling me you are lactating? And your penis has grown?"

"Well, yeah. It's normal, right? I mean, you're giving me all those hormones."

The doctor looked alarmed. "May I see your prescription bottle?"

Jay had it in his pocket. He fished it out, which took a while because it hid behind his dick. "Here you go."

The doctor read the label. "Right, Progesterone 20

mg." He opened the bottle and gasped. "There was a mistake! They gave you 200 milligrams!"

It took a moment for this to sink in. While Dale waited for the doctor to explain what it meant, he put his head in his hands. Dale started to tear up. "Does this mean we're losing the baby?"

The doctor looked up. "No, but we've never given such a high dose to a man before. Apparently, it's converting to testosterone in your system. It's causing gonad changes. Are your balls bigger, too? Let me see."

The doctor yanked Dale's pants down. Sure enough, Dale's itty bitty balls were not so itty bitty. The doctor squeezed a nipple, expressing milk. He caught it in a Petri dish to study later.

Jay spoke up. "What does this mean for Dale and the baby?"

The doctor scratched his head. "Most Dionysian sections end in stillbirth, but this is the healthiest baby I've ever seen. I am certain it's because we have always used such a low dose of progesterone. I also think most men who host a fetus in their thigh have a much higher testosterone level than you had, Dale. Forgive me, but your penis was one of the smallest I had ever seen. It's normal now. Very small, but not a micropenis."

The doctor paused to take a deep breath. Jay patted Dale on the head. "My little buddy isn't so little anymore."

Dale rolled his eyes. "Am I going to die?"

The doctor shook his head. "I don't think so. This rebalancing of your testosterone is good for you and the baby. I'm going to recommend we keep you on the high dose."

Dale said, "I don't get it. I thought progesterone was for women. Why is my testosterone level rising?"

The doctor said, "I can see why you're confused. The name progesterone in medical terms means 'supporting pregnancy,' so of course, it's associated with women. But in men, it's a precursor to testosterone. It calms nerves, increases libido, heals bones, makes tendons more flexible, and ultimately encourages the male body to generate its own sex hormones - testosterone and gonadotropins."

Dale said, "So, is that like the testosterone bodybuilders use to grow muscles?"

The doctor shrugged. "Yeah, now that you mention it. You should start lifting weights with your upper body and see what happens, but I'm sure it will encourage muscle growth. Let me check your collarbone."

The doctor moved Dale's shoulder. Dale felt no pain, so the doctor said, "I will recommend you start using this arm again. Lifting weights would be ideal. I'll send a physical therapist to help you get your routine started. I still want you to stay off that right leg, but he'll get you on a good program."

The doctor called in a male nurse to show Dale how to use crutches. After a few failed attempts, Dale got it. He realized that you have to lean on the crutch opposite the side you are supporting and swing your good leg forward. Five minutes later, they left the hospital. Dale's massive leg got many stares from passersby, but none of them could have suspected he was carrying a baby.

10

PHYSICAL THERAPY

The next morning, a knock came at the door while Jay was off changing oil and bossing mechanics around. Dale grabbed his crutches and opened the door to reveal a blond-haired, blue-eyed, cherubic young man.

"Hi, I'm Troy. The doc sent me."

"Are you my nurse?"

"Physical Therapist. I think they canceled your nurse."

Dale ushered him in. The boy walked with a wiggle. His tight shorts hugged his ass, which was eating the nylon fabric so the crack showed. With all the hormones coursing through his body, Dale was surprised when his little dick got hard. For the first time, he tented his pajamas. The thing must have grown an inch overnight! The boy saw Dale's boner, smiled, but said nothing.

"We're going to start with some basic stuff. Do you think you can do pushups without using that leg?"

Dale tried and succeeded at the unusual push-ups. He put his pregnant leg on top of the other and used both shoulders and biceps to lift off the ground. He didn't return to the ground because his hard cock got in the way. In years past, exercise like that hurt and left him feeling ill. With his new hormonal balance, it was quite the opposite. When he reached twenty reps, he kept going until he hit fifty. He was high on endorphins.

"Great work! You're gonna be sore tomorrow, but that's part of the therapy." The cherubic therapist patted Dale on the back.

"Next, we'll do some balance. Stand by the kitchen sink on your good leg. If you feel like you're going to lose it, grab the counter."

The exercise went well. Dale had no trouble balancing, even with the extra heavy leg. The baby kicked once, throwing him off balance, and he nearly fell. Troy caught him.

"Easy, tiger."

Troy bent over to remove some light dumbbells from his carrying case. The fabric of his nylon shorts stretched tight across his ass. Dale's chub started leaking. His pajamas had a little wet spot in the front. They continued with the routine. Dale worked up a sweat, giving off a powerful odor.

Troy found every excuse to bend over. Finally, he leaned in and whispered in Dale's ear. "I want you to fuck me."

His entire life, Dale never imagined hearing those words. His cock now measured at least three inches hard, maybe four. It was narrow, but it was long enough to fuck. He nearly came in his pajamas right then.

Troy knelt and pulled down the pajamas. Dale couldn't believe his eyes. The workout alone had made his cock bigger. Troy quickly slipped him into his mouth and started sucking. Dale had been licked but never sucked. Jay still saw him as a hole for his huge cock. Troy was different. When he stood and pulled down his shorts, Dale saw something amazing. Troy was hung very small. What amazed Dale was that he was much bigger than Troy. He was the top dog in this transaction.

Troy pushed Dale onto the couch and climbed into his lap. He spread his cheeks and easily sat down on Dale's small dick. He rode Dale, sliding his ass cheeks back and forth. Dale had never felt anything like it. Jacking off a one-inch cock his whole life, he'd never imagined he would feel the sensation of pushing past the inner ring. When his flared head hit Troy's prostate, the boy moaned.

"I love cocks like yours. They're all pleasure and no pain."

Dale came almost immediately, but the hormones wouldn't let his hard-on subside. Troy went for another ride that lasted a good ten minutes before Dale blew a second load inside him. Troy dismounted and put Dale's semi-hard cock in his mouth to clean off the cum. The cleaning session became a blow job, and Dale shot a third load in Troy's mouth. Troy stood and leaned into Dale, kissing him. The taste of his own cum on Troy's tongue made him hard again.

Troy said, "Sorry to leave you hanging, but our time is up. I'll be back tomorrow."

11

FLIPPING

Each day when Troy came, Dale's dick was slightly bigger. He was almost a small average now. Two weeks into the sessions, Dale heard a beautiful sound: "Ow!"

Jay was impressed by Dale's growth. He had no idea that Dale had been practicing fucking his PT. Dale felt a surge of the old feelings towards Jay, wanting to hurt him. His cock was average and thick, even soft. The more the baby swelled inside his leg, the bigger his dick got. At his next check-up, the doctor gasped. "This is a miracle! The progesterone couldn't possibly make you grow like this."

Dale said, "The bigger the baby gets, the bigger I get."

The doctor clapped his hands. "Of course! Human Growth Hormone and Testosterone from the growing boy in your leg must be somehow affecting your gonads."

Dale said, "Will it go away after I give birth?"

The doctor shook his head. "Growth like this is irreversible."

Dale would carry the fetus for another month. The baby's growth accelerated. Dale's soft cock hung down one leg now. Jay looked askance at Dale each night when he fucked him. He was uneasy now that Dale was so much bigger. Finally, one night, Dale popped the question.

"Will you let me fuck you?"

Jay shook his head. "I don't do that."

Dale added, "Yet." He lifted Jay's legs forcefully with his strong arms, biceps bulging. He tongued Jay's hole, tasting its coppery essence. His cock felt huge between his legs compared to the tiny nub he was born with.

Jay wriggled in protest, but the tongue must have felt better than he expected. His protests became soft moans.

Jay said, "No. Don't. Stop."

Dale laughed. "Okay, I won't."

Jay pushed on Dale's shoulder with his foot, but it wasn't a hard push, not enough to remove Dale's tongue from his ass. It was obvious Jay was fighting his urges. He relented and let Dale tongue him deep.

Jay said, "Does getting fucked feel this good?"

Dale nodded. "It's different. It hurts a lot, then it feels way better than this." He went back to slurping on Jay's tight asshole.

Jay said, "You're not nearly as big as me. Do you think it will hurt?"

Dale shrugged. "It will hurt, but not as bad."

Dale realized it wasn't a question in the hypothetical. He'd said "will," not "would."

Jay sighed. "Go easy on me. I'm ready. It's the least I can do for you."

Dale was at an advantage. He'd been fucked by a few different men, and he'd acquired some technique from the experience. He knew to push in the head and wait.

His muscles bulged as he got into the modified push-up, with his pregnant leg resting on the other. Leaning all his weight on one arm, he spit on his dick and massaged it with his free hand. Holding an average-sized cock where there had only been a nipple was intoxicating. He got very hard. He put the head, which was nearly as big as Jay's, at the opening. He carefully lowered himself. Jay cried out when the head started stretching the hole.

Dale waited. Jay's shallow breaths deepened as he relaxed. Dale pushed again, feeling the tight sphincter muscles pressing against the corona. With one hard push, he popped in. Jay thrashed and beat the mattress. "Take it out!"

Dale said, "Wait a few seconds. I swear it will feel good."

Jay whimpered, then relaxed. "You're right. It does."

Unlike Jay, who only got worse as he pushed deeper, Dale was a straight shot. He couldn't even reach the end of the rectum. Dale's corona rubbed against Jay's prostate as he see-sawed in his hole. Jay's eyes fluttered. "Oh, shit. I had no idea. This is fucking great!"

Dale was careful not to pull out too far. Jay would push him out like a turd if he let his corona pass the inner sphincter. He moved in shallow strokes, rubbing Jay's sweet spot until the giant cock stood straight up in front of Dale, leaking a small fountain of clear, sticky juice. Dale lapped it up greedily. His tongue sent Jay into a spasm. Dale felt the sphincter squeeze and release him repeatedly. It was too much.

"Oh shit, Jay, I'm gonna cum."

Jay held Dale by the waist, pulling him inside all the way. "Nut in me."

By now, Jay's towering appendage was throbbing. The flow of pre-cum stopped. It waggled in the air, straining. Jay put a hand at the base and gently rubbed it.

Dale couldn't hold back. He put the tip of Jay's cock in his mouth and released a massive flood of sperm in his asshole.

Jay said, "It's so warm. Oh shit. Here it comes."

The first squirt filled Dale's mouth. He leaned back

to swallow. Jay erupted repeatedly, filling the air with his cum, which rained down on both men. Their hair, faces, necks, and bodies were wet with Jay's musky seed.

Jay's eyes burned with hunger. "I've never felt this close to anyone, not even your sister." He pulled Dale to his lips, and they explored each other's mouths until they were hard again. Dale took less time the second time. He was so turned on by all that had happened that it immediately made him blow another big load in Jay's ass. He then clamped his mouth over Jay's pole and rammed it down his throat, fucking it with his tonsils until it gave him a nourishing flood of semen.

Jay carried Dale to the bed, where they cuddled and fucked until late into the night.

12

LABOR PAINS

After that night, the two men took turns pleasuring each other and getting pleasure in return. The long days while Jay was away, Troy engulfed Dale's ever-growing cock. At eight-and-a-half months, the baby was an enormous lump, stretching Dale's thigh so much that the skin was translucent in certain spots. One day, the baby shifted. Dale was in excruciating pain. Every time the baby kicked, he howled aloud. Troy called Jay at work.

Jay asked, "What is it?"

Troy said, "I don't know, Dale's in a lot of pain. I think I'm going to take him to the hospital if that's okay."

"Please do! I'll head over there now."

Dale writhed in agony on the trip to the medical center. Whenever he stopped at a light, Troy patted his head, massaged his neck, or rubbed his belly.

Dale spoke through gritted teeth. "Touch my cock, rub it a little."

Troy reached down and felt the decent-sized cock swelling under his fingers.

"That helps." Dale's breathing grew more regular. "Take it out and play with it."

Troy drove one-handed, jerking Dale as they sped

through town. A half mile from the hospital, a siren blasted. A cop car pulled out of a blind alley. The car's loudspeaker crackled. "Pull over."

The cop stepped out of his cruiser and approached Troy's little Ford Fiesta. Dale struggled to put away his hard cock, but it got jammed in the zipper.

The cop removed his sunglasses and leaned into the window. "What's going on here? Do you know how fast you were going?"

Troy pleaded with the cop. "My friend here is dying. I'm trying to get him to the hospital."

"Dying for you to jack him off?"

Dale spoke. "It helps with the pain."

The officer's dark blue polyester pants caught the light, revealing a huge, thick cock running down one leg. "I'll escort you to the hospital as a favor, but then you gotta do me a solid in return."

Troy nodded. "Yes, sir, officer."

The cop blasted his siren and escorted the men the last half mile to the County Medical Center.

Jay was waiting, bewildered and sick with worry. "What happened?"

The cop spoke up. "I pulled them over. Sorry for the delay."

An orderly came out with a gurney and helped Dale onto it. The cop followed Troy and Jay into the hospital. He cupped Troy's perky ass and whispered to him. "Don't forget, I need the favor returned."

Troy blushed. Jay was far too worried about Dale to notice the interaction between the two men. Jay accompanied Dale to the ultrasound. A nurse asked him about their relationship.

"He's carrying my baby."

She paused to process the strange information. "I heard about you. You're his brother-in-law, right?"

Jay nodded. She made a tick mark in her notepad. "Come on."

They wheeled Dale into the exam room for an ultrasound. His doctor joined them. Dale groaned with pain as the technician rubbed the wand over the affected area. The nurse set up an IV drip and added painkillers. Dale grew docile and quiet.

The doctor said, "Dale has had too much movement, it seems. The baby has shifted, and it's pressing on a lot of new nerves and causing dangerous muscle contractions. We will have to ask Dale to stay very still in a bed here for the next fourteen days until we can perform the Dionysian section."

Jay looked heartbroken. "Can't he stay at home?"

Dale was too dopey to care. "It's cool, Jay. I can hang here."

The orderly rolled the gurney upstairs to a private bedroom paid for by the research foundation monitoring Dale's pregnancy. If this baby were born, it would be the first of its kind, and many eyes were on Dale.

By the next morning, the pain had subsided. By not having vigorous sex all day and all night, he could adapt to the baby's new position. His muscle contractions died down, and he was able to sleep.

Over the next two weeks, dozens of visiting medical professors stopped by to examine Dale, ask questions, and poke and prod. Dale grew annoyed by the endless interviews and exams, but he knew it was for an important scientific cause, so he remained polite and cooperative.

Jay visited him every day. He often brought Troy along.

Dale was curious. "What happened with that cop?"

Troy blushed. "We're dating. He's huge. I can't hear my farts anymore."

Dale forgot that his affair with Troy was clandestine. "He's a lot bigger than me, I suppose."

Troy didn't answer. He looked silently from Dale to Jay.

Dale added, "Not that you would know." But it was too late. The cat was out of the bag.

Jay chuckled. "I knew you were up to something. But Troy's so little, how can he fuck you?"

Now, it was Dale's turn to be shocked. "How do you know that?"

Jay blushed. "Come on, an ass like that. I couldn't stay out of it."

Troy clarified. "Yeah, I'm a slut. I take all comers. Jay is a lot more than I'm used to, but I can take him. Dale's got enough, and he's getting bigger by the hour."

It was true. As the baby's growth accelerated, Dale's cock reached the high end of average. It was almost "big."

The men stared at each other in a crackling hot silence. The air was charged with sexual energy. Silently, Jay closed the door to the suite. He pulled the curtain for added privacy.

Troy bent over the bed, his face hovering above Dale's soft cock, which he put into his mouth. It quickly grew until it pressed on Troy's tonsils. Meanwhile, Jay pulled down Troy's tight corduroys, exposing the big, perfect ass. There was a big tube of KY jelly in the nightstand drawer. Jay slicked up his massive cock and plunged it quickly into Troy, snaking his way past the inner door in one go.

Troy suppressed a scream. He was loose, but not enough to take that much in such a short time.

"Wait," he said, putting a hand on Jay's thigh.

Jay waited. Troy went back to slurping on Dale's plump cock. He choked as it pushed past his tonsils, but he used his neck like a pump handle to bounce up and down, taking Dale's full length down his throat.

Troy pulled up for air. "Okay, go."

Jay got the signal. He started to pump slowly, gaining speed. Troy's mouth was full, so his words came out as grunts and moans.

Dale was able to stay still despite the incredible sensations coursing through his full-sized cock. Troy swirled his tongue over the head like a greedy child with an ice cream cone. He watched his lover plowing Troy's backside. He yearned to have his ass stuffed but knew the baby was more important. When Troy pinched a nipple, milk squirted into his hair. The cocksucker pulled up and laughed, spraying milk into his mouth.

"Holy shit, that's like the best drug I've ever had."

He went back down on Dale, sucking enthusiastically. Jay increased the pace of his thrusts, causing Troy to tremble inside. He bucked at the waist, unable to control the orgasmic contractions. With his mouth full, he said, "Oh, shit." His little penis began to drip, then gush with cum. It stained the edge of the bed.

Jay couldn't see but knew he'd pushed Troy over the edge. He wanted to do it again. He sped up and banged his balls against Troy's thighs repeatedly. Troy doubled over from pleasure, building to a second orgasm. He never lost concentration, sucking Dale's cock with single-minded purpose.

Dale felt a swelling in his balls, and then they began to lift off the bed. "I'm coming."

Troy pulled back, jerking Dale's cock with one hand. At least two inches were poking past the blurred fist as it pumped up and down.

Mindful to keep still, Dale leaned his head back and let out a stifled cry. His cock shot cum into the air in huge spoonfuls. Troy gasped at his handiwork.

"Oh fuck, that's hot. I'm gonna —" He didn't finish. He closed his eyes and moaned. Another heavy load shot from his miniature penis. This time, Jay saw it, and it put him over the edge.

"Oh fuck! It's here." Jay threw his head back and let out a loud sigh. Dale could see Jay's balls pulsing like a bee stinger, pumping cum, not venom, into Troy's broad backside. He collapsed on top of the physical therapist, drenched with sweat. Dale caressed Troy's ears and ran his finger through his hair. Then he touched Troy's cheek.

Dale said, "I fucking needed that."

Troy and Jay simultaneously replied, "Me, too."

13

LOVING FATHERS

Nine months after Dale's sister conceived Jay's child and two months after the fetus was implanted in Dale's thigh, the doctors wheeled Dale into the operating room. Jay paced anxiously in the waiting room while the nurses prepped Dale for surgery. They wheeled him into an operating theater, where dozens of surgeons, gynecologists, and other medical professionals sat in seats around the table. You could hear a pin drop. The anticipation was palpable.

Dale looked around the room in dismay. They'd neglected to tell him that his birth would have an audience. Before he could protest, a nurse placed a face mask over his mouth and added something to his IV. He felt fuzzy, and the room began to fade.

While Dale slept, the doctors extracted the healthy baby from his leg. They neatly sewed him up, and wheeled him into the recovery room.

Jay, who'd feared the worst, was horrified when the doctor walked out frowning. But the scene changed. The doctor said, "Congratulations, you're the father of a healthy baby girl." He escorted Jay to the recovery room, where Dale was just waking up.

"Hi." Jay shifted from one foot to the other.

"Hey." Dale winced when he moved. His leg was

tender and would need many more hours of Troy's time to get back in shape.

Jay bent down and kissed Dale on the lips. A few nurses scoffed, but the doctor smiled. "I'm glad this experience has formed a bond between you two. Not everyone approves of two men raising a child, but I do."

A young candy striper brought in the baby and handed it to Dale. He held the infant to his chest. The tiny girl was asleep, no doubt exhausted from the experience of being plucked from Dale's thigh. Dale handed the girl to Jay, who rocked her gently as she slept. They were such good friends that they scarcely needed words to share their love, delight, and joy as new parents.

"She's beautiful." Jay had tears in his eyes.

Dale nodded.

They marveled at their child until the candy striper came to bring her back to the neonatal unit.

Dale reached between his legs to ensure everything he'd gained remained there. It was even more than he remembered. He was a good four inches soft. His balls had turned from tiny peas into walnuts. He realized he might be too big for Jay now. It would be pure irony if it were true.

The doctor interrupted Dale's penis dreams. "Have you picked out a name for her?"

Jay and Dale looked at each other dumbfounded. They hadn't.

They decided on Marla Clark-Benson in honor of the late mother, Dale's sister. She would never know her mother, but Marla could at least live with her name and the last names of her two fathers.

Dale was a pro when it came to crutches. He shooed away the orderly who tried to help him to his feet. Jay carried Marla, and Dale hobbled quickly down the hallway, anxious to put the hospital in his rear-view mirror.

When he got home, he was astonished. Jay had created a nursery out of the spare bedroom. They laid

Marla in her crib. She was a quiet baby, thankfully. When she woke, she didn't cry for milk; she just cooed. As soon as Dale heard the sounds, his nipples leaked. He fed Marla until she knocked out.

Dale's ass was hungrier than his leg was sore. He needed Jay inside him. They retired to their bedroom, where Dale lay on his left side with his right leg on a pillow. Jay fucked him sideways, which always felt the best. The tall hole on its side became wide, and Jay's cock was very, very thick. Masterfully, Jay plunged deep inside his lover, caressing his insides with his fat cock. Dale ignored the pain in his thigh. The sensations were too good to stop and take a pain pill.

When Dale felt the warm cum fill him, he breathed a sigh of relief. Deep in the recesses of his consciousness, he feared that Jay would lose interest in him as soon as the child was born. It wasn't true. If anything, Jay was more devoted than ever.

The following day, news reporters trampled the lawn. Even though there was doctor-patient confidentiality, it appears it didn't extend to the witnesses at Dale's Dionysian section. Jay came out on the porch, Marla in his arms, and quieted the reporters.

"Dale's recovering. Can you please give us some peace and quiet?"

A reporter shouted, "The Southern Baptist Convention has condemned your child's birth as Satanic. What do you have to say to them?"

Jay shrugged. "Hail, Satan? I doubt the devil had anything to do with it. Marla is a miracle, not a curse."

Dale came to the door on crutches, and the reporters went wild.

"What was it like carrying a baby as a man?"

"Did it hurt?"

"What is your relationship with the father?"

The questions were unrelenting. Dale waved and smiled. He made a quieting gesture.

"I'm in love with this man." He put an arm around Jay. "And I'm pretty sure he's in love with me."

They looked into each other's eyes. Jay nodded. They kissed. Cameras flashed, reporters murmured, but the moment was such a genuine expression of true love that a hushed silence followed. Love takes many faces. Love walks on many different legs. Dale and Jay were lucky enough to share the bond many lonely people never find. And they shared their love of a child they both fathered, which was unique in this world.

EPILOGUE

Dale's cock was big. It hung four inches soft, seven-and-a-half when it was hard. It was as big around as a pork tenderloin. Jay asked for it all the time. Dale was happy to give it to him, but he preferred to lay back and let Jay fuck him. They took turns swapping two or three times a night. With each dumped load of cum, the bond between the men grew stronger. Soon, they were as close as two men could ever be.

Jay craved the milk from Dale's nipples. He was greedy enough that Dale had to stop him so Marla could have her share. When it was time to wean Marla, Jay refused to let the milk dry up. Dale relented, and Jay enjoyed the milk for many more years until, at last, it ran dry.

THE EXPECTANT
MEMBER

FOREWORD BY THE AUTHOR

Some day a transgendered male will conceive and give birth. This is inevitable. The hormones, no matter how masculine they make the subject, will not always win out over the vitality of fertility.

What really may never come to pass is a phallic pregnancy. I have speculated and imagined a manner in which it could occur, but the medical details are ridiculous. What is probably based more on factual circumstances is the veil of secrecy such a pregnancy would demand. Of course, Central Intelligence would poke, prod, and pester a man half to death in an effort to determine how it happened and how it could be repeated. Such is the scientific method.

America is a nation that prides itself on its freedom. What we have learned is that freedom is an ideal, not a reality. Only a few years ago, I was not free to kiss another man, let alone sleep with him. I had to claim that freedom for myself, away from the prying eyes of an illegitimate authority. Even today, with homosexuality being decriminalized and depathologized, we face resistance. Our love cannot be sanctioned with marriage. Be grateful for the small freedoms we have, and imagine a world with more. Perhaps we can make our dreams a reality.

— PETER SCHUTES, SANTA MONICA,
CA. 1978

❧ I ❧

MILO

My name is Milo, and I had Ectopic Phallogeniasis. This is my story.

Sex was always a sport for me. Having a cock of horse proportions made things challenging, but I always found a willing hole. Men seemed to like getting fucked by me more than women. Women often cried, eventually asking me to stop. Men, especially the athletic types, were more into the pain. They pounded the mattress and bit the pillow, but they endured. I guess I prefer them now, but I won't turn away a size queen if she's willing to stick with it.

Most of my sexual encounters happened during my lunch hour. I worked around the corner from a North Hollywood bathhouse with a businessman's special. Two hours for ten dollars and all the ass you could fuck.

It was on a noontime break that I met Jordan. He was so handsome; I gasped the first time I saw him. I saw his tiny penis and nonexistent balls, and I just had to fuck him.

Lucky for me, Jordan was a fan of the big ones. When we got to his room, I got the shock of my life. Jordan had undergone surgery to alter from female to male. His penis was an enlarged clitoris. He had a vagina where his balls would have been. He lay on his back, fingering his pussy, expecting rejection. When I took off my sweatpants, revealing the mammoth, he sucked air through his teeth.

"Holy fuck, dude, that's a friggin' monster!"

I was just as sure of rejection. "Yeah, I mean, I get it." I started to put it away.

"Fuck me! Please!" Jordan spread his hairy legs wide, pulling apart his pussy lips. I think if I were utterly gay, that would have made me feel queasy. Instead, it awoke new perversions in my already filthy mind. I wanted him; he wanted me.

"I don't wear condoms. They don't fit."

"I don't give a fuck. I'm on hormones. I can't get pregnant."

His vagina wasn't tight, but it was shallow. I hit the bottom near the cervix when I was only half in. I had to hold my cock above the base to avoid injuring him.

Jordan was insatiable. On his back, he watched my thick meat stretch his belly as I filled his hole to bursting. Every time my cock hit the cervix, he jumped.

"Am I hurting you?"

Jordan shook his head. It felt good, so I kept rubbing at the cervix, freaking out at how good it felt to be inside a man's pussy. A real pussy.

Jordan wrapped his legs around my waist, pulling me so close my cock started to double back on itself.

"Oh fuck, Milo! That's it. Right there."

Jordan quivered with orgasm. The contractions in his cunt squeezed my cock hard so that when I came, the first few spurts didn't come out. They felt like they went backward. Then I pulled back and let out a flood of sperm in Jordan's vagina. Dripping with sweat, I lay on top of the trans man, feeling his heartbeat on my chest. When I pulled out, no cum came. It was all either up inside Jordan or trapped somewhere in my dick.

Neither of us knew that we'd just had historical sex. That moment changed both of our lives forever.

I usually prefer my sex anonymous, but something about the young trans man made me want to be more than just a lay. I felt the first stirrings of love. I'd never had love, so I didn't recognize it. I just thought I wanted to fuck him again. So, we exchanged numbers.

We met almost daily at the baths. I still had my guard up. I wasn't ready to let Jordan into my bachelor life. But each time we fucked, it got more intense. We started kissing. For a few weeks, it was my daily fix. Then, one day, he didn't show up, so I called him.

"Jordan, it's almost 1 pm. Are you coming?"

"I don't feel good. I think I got food poisoning."

My protective instincts took over. "Do you need anything?"

Jordan said, "Can you just come over and massage my temples?"

I took the subway downtown to his loft. Jordan never told me what he did, but judging by the furnishings in his place, he was well compensated. Or perhaps he had a trust fund. My bachelor pad in Van Nuys was far below his standards.

A thin sheen of sweat coated Jordan's face. His brown eyes locked with mine. I held his head in my lap and massaged his scalp and temples.

Jordan purred. "I love you, Milo."

The words every bachelor dreads hung in the air for a split second. Something came over me. "I love you, too." I kissed his perfect lips and rubbed his flat chest.

The next day, I was sick. I puked my guts out. I must have caught the stomach flu from Jordan. But it didn't feel like food poisoning or flu. I just felt a powerful wave of nausea that sometimes won out and caused me to vomit.

I also felt a twinge of pain when I peed. Maybe Jordan had given me the clap. I didn't want to jump to conclusions. I went to the VD clinic for a checkup.

Doctor Minty took my blood and asked me dozens

of screening questions. He did a digital rectal exam to confirm my prostate was normal.

"Milo, I'm not sure what is causing your symptoms. I'll call you when the blood tests come back. It definitely isn't the clap."

A day later, the phone rang. It was Doctor Minty. "Milo? I need you to come back down. We need to retest you right away."

Shit. Fuck. It was cancer, I was sure. But what I heard that day at the clinic blew my mind.

❧ 2 ❦

HCG

I sat in the swivel chair, unwilling to hear what Minty was telling me.

"Why would you even test for that?"

Dr. Minty explained. "Milo, we have a contract with a local lab that offers a discount if we run all the blood and urine through the same panel. It includes HCG."

HCG. Human Chorionic Gonadotropin. The hormone that a fetus releases.

"What kind of cancer would cause me to produce HCG?" I tried to cover my terror with cool, logical questions.

Minty frowned. "See, that's just it. No cancer causes elevated HCG levels in men. They can only be produced by an embryo. I think I should refer you to the UCLA Endocrine Center for further tests."

"I'm not sure my insurance will cover it."

Minty laughed. "They're not going to charge you. If anything, they'll pay you for further studies."

When I got home, I vacillated between fear and curiosity. What the fuck was going on? The phone rang.

It was my fuck buddy, Jordan. He was born with a pussy, but he's had the top surgery and takes testosterone, so he's a guy as far as I'm concerned. He has an extra hole, that's all.

Jordan said, "Uh, hi, Milo."

"Jordan? What's up? Are you feeling better?"

"I just found out I'm pregnant. I think you're the father."

The human body is unpredictable. I had a sexual response. My cock lifted off my leg and strained at my pants leg.

"That's great!"

"Dude, I'm a man. I'm a pregnant man. How is that great?"

"It means we're going to be parents."

Jordan said, "I was going to get an abortion."

That hurt to hear. It was his choice, of course, but I was the father of that child. "Will you reconsider?"

Jordan hung up. Then he called back. "Sorry, I had a lot to process."

I said, "It's cool."

Jordan sighed. "I guess it's cool. I feel bad for the kid. He's going to have a hard time. His mom's a dude... and single."

"You could marry."

"Who's going to marry a pregnant man? Is it even legal?"

"Why not? What does your birth certificate say? You're female. I'm male."

There was a long pause. "You're asking me to marry you?"

I couldn't believe how the paternal instinct was driving me to reckless love statements. "Jordan Greer, will you marry me?"

The phone went silent. Then he said, "This is all happening so fast."

I said, "Well, I'm here for you, no matter what you decide."

"Can I come over?"

❧

Jordan sat cross-legged on the ottoman. He eyed my thigh hungrily. My monster was trapped under corduroy, plastered to my mid-thigh, straining to get out.

"The doctor said I could have sex." Jordan put his hand between his legs and rubbed his big clitoris.

I didn't need an invitation. I stood up and removed my T-shirt in one move. My pants came off with some difficulty, but at last, the monster swung skyward, fighting gravity with the vim and vigor of youth. Jordan pushed me onto the sofa and straddled my cock, putting the head in his pussy before squatting to his knees. My cock swelled bigger than I ever remembered it. Jordan's cunt stretched to accommodate my increased girth. The length was the same, but it was still too long. Jordan bounced up and down on his knees, preventing the last five or six inches from getting inside him. His enlarged clit coated my cock with its sticky effluence. I put my hand on it and rubbed vigorously. Jordan's eyes rolled back in his head.

"Oh God! Milo! Keep doing that, please!" The more I rubbed, the stickier it got. Then in a total surprise, it retracted and spit out a gob of cum. Just like a real dick.

My hips began to thrust upward of their own accord, banging my cock hard into the bottom of Jordan's pussy. Jordan adjusted, coming up straight on his knees, giving me room to thrust without hurting him.

Jordan came again; the juices gathered in my belly button. Nobody else in the world could have sex like this. We were a perfect pair. I felt my love grow with each needy thrust.

I felt my balls tighten, a sure sign I was close.

"Jordan, I'm gonna come."

"Do it, Milo, fill my pussy."

And I did. Knowing I was coming inside the father of my baby made it even better. But I felt an ache or cramp at the base of my cock, which continued to hurt after I pulled out. My cock was swollen and purple. It wouldn't go down.

Jordan drove me to UCLA Medical Center Emergency.

The nurse reassured me. "Hon, this is priapism. We see it every day. You got sickle cell anemia?"

"No."

"Do you take any medications? Did a spider bite you?"

I never heard such an odd assortment of questions. Thankfully, the doctor came and shooed the nurse away. He took one look at my swollen cock, which was ordinarily huge but now was gigantic, and said, "I'm going to operate."

The next thing I remember, I woke up with a drain coming out of my mid-shaft. Jordan stood when he saw me stir.

"What happened?"

Jordan explained. "Something was blocking your dorsal vein so that the blood couldn't escape. They drained the blood."

I gagged, thinking about it. But the pressure in my cock, which had been building slowly over the past couple of weeks, felt much better.

"Did they find out what's blocking the vein?"

They didn't say.

The doctor came back into the room. He lifted my gown and nodded approvingly.

"You're improving. We'll have this drain out in a jiffy."

I said, "What caused it?"

He shrugged. "It could be any number of causes, including causes we don't even know about yet."

They could never have guessed the cause.

ULTRASOUND

Jordan had to go to work. I was already at UCLA Hospital, so Dr. Paul, the endocrinologist, came to me and took some blood. He ran it through a battery of tests and returned a few hours later scratching his head.

"It is most certainly HCG and the levels are higher than last week."

"And it's not cancer?"

Dr. Paul laughed. "No, relax. Even with testicular cancer, you wouldn't have such elevated levels. Something's off, but it's not cancer."

"How do you know?"

Dr. Paul said, "To ease your mind, I'll have the radiology team do an ultrasound on your genitals and a scan of your pituitary gland."

The young man who showed up with the portable ultrasound was not prepared to have so much surface area to cover.

"Jesus, man, that's the biggest dick I ever seen."

I smiled at the compliment. I never got tired of people admiring my big dick. He rubbed cold gel along the length of my penis and all over my balls. He chuckled.

"Usually, this takes less than three minutes." He

checked his watch. "It's been ten minutes, and we haven't even started the ultrasound yet."

All the rubbing had an unfortunate side effect. My cock started to swell.

"Sorry, man, you just keep rubbing it."

The technician said, "No sweat. It's better if you have a semi. Don't worry."

The technician started the rhythmic spiraling journey from the tip of my cock to the base. He frowned near the base.

"What? What is it?"

"Sorry. I'm not supposed to interpret what I'm seeing."

"Is it cancer?"

"Probably not, but that's all I'm going to say. Let the doctors give the diagnosis. I could lose my job."

He squeezed my balls at the top of the sack and ran the wand slowly around the circumference. I could swear he was trying to turn me on. When his pinky strayed and touched my taint, I knew he was.

The technician cupped my balls and licked the tip of my dick. He opened his mouth and managed to put the first four inches in. When I hit his tonsils, I could tell he was inexperienced. I had met talented cock-suckers who could take the whole shaft. This guy was an amateur.

Still, it felt good with two hands on the bottom seven and his mouth on the rest. He leaked some of that special spit I call 'stomach juice,' the kind you only get from giving head. His hands got wet, becoming like an extension of his mouth. I closed my eyes and pretended I was fucking Jordan in the ass. He hadn't let me go there yet. I know pussy is a lot wider, but it's not as deep. Between the technician's mouth and his hands, it felt like I was buried completely in some tight wet ass. I lay back and let the ultrasound guy finish what he started.

In a few minutes, my balls started to gurgle. The technician sucked and slurped, cupping my churning sac and squeezing it like he was trying to get a single drop out of a giant eye dropper. When he put his pinky in my asshole, I came unraveled.

"I'm gonna— "There was no time to finish. A sharp pain at the base of my cock made me cry out. Then the floodgates opened. The poor guy had his work cut out for him. He swallowed a half dozen spurts of my come before he gave up and let the rest hit his face and uniform. The last droplets rolled down my fat cock head and made the long journey to my pubes.

"Was the pain because of the drain?"

"Pain? You felt pain?"

I pointed to the base. "Right here."

"We drained your mid-shaft. A little pain is normal at the site but not down there. Be sure to tell Doctor Paul."

৩৯৫

LIKE EVERY MAN WHO SEES MY COCK, DOCTOR PAUL made an audible gasp when I uncovered it for him.

"If there's pain, we need to involve a urologist as well. But I've studied your ultrasound, and I'm afraid I don't have answers. It can't be what it looks like, but it isn't cancer."

I felt like a pass-around Patty. The urologist said he needed to make a referral after examining the ultrasound. After hours of poking and prodding, the new doctor showed up.

He was tall and handsome, a real Daddy type. He sat beside me. I saw his name tag read Dr. Litchfield, OB.GYN. What was a gynecologist doing with a dick problem?

"The results of the ultrasound are clear. There's no

medical explanation for it, Milo, but you have an extremely rare condition called Ectopic Phallogeniasis."

"Is it deadly?"

Dr. Litchfield said, "Not if we treat it."

"What is it, exactly?"

The doctor hesitated. "You have an ectopic pregnancy in your urethra."

My head spun around like the Exorcist. I felt dizzy. "What the fuck is an ectopic pregnancy, and what is it doing in my dick?"

Dr. Litchfield said, "Ectopic is any pregnancy outside of a uterus. You have no uterus, so our best bet is that, somehow, a fertilized egg got into your bladder. Perhaps through retrograde ejaculation."

I thought about my first time having sex with Jordan two months ago. I remembered those first three spurts that didn't come out. My dick was so tightly wedged against his cervix the cum shot in the other direction, which hurt like a motherfucker. Those last few spurts stayed inside him. They probably went straight up into his uterus, which is how he got pregnant despite his hormone therapy.

"I think I had retro—retrograde ejaculation about two months ago."

"Was it with a woman?" The doctor took notes.

"Well, sort of. It was a guy, but he used to be a girl, and he still has his pu— his vagina."

"FTM." The doctor was scribbling in loud strokes.

He continued to ask me a series of questions that helped make sense of an absurd situation. We figured it out.

I was stretching Jordan's cervix, which caused him to release an extra egg that somehow made it down my pee hole. When I shot half my load into my bladder, the egg went along for the ride and was fertilized. The next time I pissed, the zygote must have traveled out of the bladder into my urethra, where it attached itself.

It's an eight-week embryo blocking my urethra. But unlike most men, I have a very long, thick cock. My urethra was wide enough to allow urine and semen to pass.

The test also showed a high level of cortisol, a hormone that causes skin to sag. The embryo was sucking up collagen but leaving elastin behind. My cock was basically a rubber band now.

Dr. Litchfield wanted me to stay the night for observation.

"Can you operate to get it out?"

The doctor grew pensive. "Are you certain you want to remove the fetus?"

"Yeah, it's not illegal or anything, is it? My life is at stake here."

Then, a strange feeling washed over me. I think many people get this when they find out they're expecting. I wanted to keep the baby. For a confirmed bachelor like me, this was a revelation.

I leaned in. "Can this baby survive?"

"If the cortisol continues to work, there's a slim chance that you can bring this baby to term. It won't be easy."

He was undoubtedly correct.

I called Jordan. "Uh, I have some news."

Jordan said, "Oh no. Is it cancer?"

"No. It's much stranger. Almost embarrassing"

"You don't have to tell me if you don't want to."

I sighed. "I kind of have to. You're going to have twins. One in your belly and one in my dick."

It was challenging to explain Ectopic Phallogeniasis, which was even more bizarre than a pregnant man with female parts.

Jordan finally understood. "Does this mean we can't fuck?"

I laughed. "The doctor didn't seem to think it would be a problem. The embryo is fully attached, and my dick is stretching to accommodate life. I might get priapism again, but I could get that just from morning wood. Sex is no riskier."

Dr. Litchfield discharged me the following day. "Keep in touch. I need you to come in at least three times a week."

"But I work."

"I'll write you a letter. Don't worry, I won't tell them you're pregnant."

$\maltese$ 4 $\maltese$

AT THE BATHS

I ended up going on disability. I was free to go to the baths any time I liked. Jordan's pregnancy had reduced his sex drive, so I cheated. In the third month, the lump in my shaft had swollen enough to make my dick impossibly thick. It was like a snake that swallowed a rat. As the weeks passed, the rat became a weasel, then a cat. Everyone at the baths wanted to worship my gargantuan pregnant cock, but none of them could take me. That was when I learned to enjoy being fucked.

It started with a stunt double named Hal. He had sleepy eyes and a great body. He saw me standing by my door, my obese cock dangling to my knee.

He said, "That's one fucking big dick. I do stunts, but that one is too dangerous."

I shrugged. "Move on, then."

Hal said, "Don't you like to get fucked? I like to play with big ones when I'm fucking."

It had been so long since I saw any real action. I ushered him into my room and closed the door. "I'm a total top, so don't tell anyone."

The stuntman laughed. "What happens at the baths is no one's secret to tell. My wife would be upset."

I laughed.

He pulled out a larger-than-average cock. It wasn't terribly thick. "You've gotten fucked before, right?

I nodded.

"Have you ever enjoyed it?"

I shook my head.

Hal grinned. Well, that's a challenge I can take on. You are going to beg me for more.

The secret, of course, was patience. He put the tip in, and I felt pain. He waited, then pressed a little more. Just when I thought my ass couldn't take any more stretching, his corona popped through the ring. The rest of the journey to fill my rectum was smooth and painless. He pulled back just enough to pop the corona out, then pushed back in. It started to feel good. As he moved his fat head back and forth over my prostate, I felt a gurgling. A little rivulet of clear precum dribbled out of my cock onto the mattress. Then, it kept dribbling until it became a long, sticky stream.

Hal said, "You like this?"

I nodded.

"Ready for me to cut loose?"

I wasn't sure what that would be and didn't care. I never understood why guys liked to get fucked, but Hal was teaching me. I nodded.

The stunt double humped me hard, squeezing my cock right where the baby was growing. I moved his hand down to the very base to protect my unborn child. He used it like a handrail to steady himself and pull closer. His strokes were the full length of his dick. The head popped in and out, giving me shivers. He was just the right size for fucking a newbie. Each stroke was pure delight. When I fucked guys, their faces were constantly screwed up in pain. I was just one big smile. It's hard being huge. This guy was lucky.

His fast rhythmic strokes in my ass matched the

pace of his hand on the base of my dick. It brought me to the edge.

"I'm gonna come."

Hal grinned. "Me too."

As my cum shot skyward, raining down like fire sprinklers, Hal unburdened himself in my ass. When he got soft, I pushed him out, then farted a slick puddle of cum.

"See, I never back down from a challenge." He kissed my forehead, a signal that this was a one-time thing. He left me wanting more.

I no longer stood at the door to my room, a sign that I was looking for a bottom to fuck. Instead, I lay on my back, my cock dangling off my hip. That position demonstrated that my dick was too big to fuck with. Instead, my hole was on display. I marveled at the number of men who wanted to fuck me. Some were small, most were normal-sized, and a few precious cocks were huge. The huge ones always made me cum without touching myself. I liked the small ones because they spent all their time bumping up next to my prostate. The normal ones were only as good as their owners. But the huge cocks, they were the holy grail. Now I understood why so many men wanted me to fuck them. If a huge cock felt terrific, mine must be like heaven to the right bottom.

As the pregnancy progressed, my already massive cock became an elephant's trunk, then an anaconda, then an anaconda that ate an elephant. It hurt my back to carry the heavy meat around.

✿ 5 ✿

JAKE THE SNAKE

Jordan and I got married at Van Nuys Civic Center. He shaved and wore a dress and makeup to minimize confusion at the registrar. He looked fine as a woman but didn't want to look pretty. He was a man. The vagina was just a biological mishap. But we both wanted to get married.

Jordan knew what was going on at the baths. Whatever jealousy he felt, he put aside in the interest of keeping us both happy. Sex isn't the defining feature of a relationship. For us, a surprise home-cooked meal or a nice back rub defined what a real relationship was about. And, of course, the impending joy of parenthood helped us along.

As Jordan's belly swelled, my cock ballooned. The embryo was long and narrow enough to really fill out the middle portion of my cock. The doctor said it could get painful, but it never did. My cock just kept swelling and stretching to accommodate the child. The only pain was in my lower back. Jordan and I often went to the OB/GYN together to save time. Technically, these two were fraternal twins, so it made sense to monitor them both as one pregnancy.

Jordan's pregnancy was unusual; mine was unprecedented. The doctors couldn't tell me what to expect.

They were just as shocked as I was when I started to express milk. That was a big hit at the baths. Guys got off on fucking me, sucking my dick, and nursing from my nipples. Word spread.

A mechanic named Jake was the culprit who ruined anal sex with anyone smaller. His nickname, not surprisingly, was Jake the Snake. He had a massive pecker between his thick thighs. He handed me some poppers and told me to inhale deeply several times. By the time my head stopped pounding, he was halfway inside me. His cock stopped at the back of my rectum. He lifted my right leg to twist me, and his cock poked through to a place I had never known existed. It kept going, snaking its way through my insides. I could see the monstrous head pressing against my belly from the inside. As he fucked me, I watched the head slide back and forth in my innards.

"Oh fuck! Oh, Jesus! Keep doing that. Right there. Just there."

Jake smiled with the confidence of a man who knew how to fuck with skill and dexterity. I had always plowed inside without a second thought about which direction to point it.

"I heard something about milk." His eyes glinted.

I squeezed a nipple, producing a droplet. He leaned forward and clamped onto my tit, sucking it hard. Each mouthful of milk gave him renewed energy. Soon he was fucking me so hard he was going to burst me open.

My cock climbed skyward, forcing its way between me and Jake. Jake pushed it out of the way and continued sucking on me. He absently started to stroke it. Then the baby kicked.

"What the fuck was that?"

I was afraid the truth would cut things short, but it was better than lies. "I got knocked up in my dick. That's the baby."

Jake said, "Oh god, that's so fucking hot." He

rubbed the baby through my cock, making it kick again and again. The kicks felt so good that they brought me to orgasm. With my baby kicking and twitching inside, my cock splattered cum on Jake's jeans.

Jake flooded my colon with his cum. I could feel the warm liquid spurting inside me. Jake pulled out still hard, causing me to yelp when the impossibly large head popped out. No wonder he gave me poppers. He finished in my hair and face, coating me with glaze.

Jake was new to the baths, but he made regular visits to see me there. He taught me techniques to bring home to Jordan. Our sex life improved when I taught Jordan to take it in the butt. I used just the first five inches of my cock, where the baby hadn't invaded yet. With that new skill in my bag of tricks, we were able to keep our sex life alive during our pregnancies.

NOSY SHEILA

Jordan had his mammary glands removed and his nipple trimmed and reattached as part of the mastectomy, so they couldn't produce milk. Luckily, my breasts were swollen with milk. I would nurse both babies. For now, I just let Jordan suck on my titties to keep the milk flowing. If we skipped a day, it would hurt. So, I kept Jordan fed on a steady diet of male breast milk.

Our frequent visits to UCLA Medical Center attracted unwanted attention. Even though our medical records were protected, somebody on staff broke in and photocopied ours. The press probably paid a small fortune for the lead. One day in our sixth month, I answered the phone.

"Is Jordan or Milo there?"

"This is Milo. How can I help you?"

The voice grew excited. "My name is Sheila, and I'm a reporter with the LA Times. Is it true that you and your wife are both pregnant?"

"Jordan is my husband."

"So, you're both pregnant, right?"

I said, "Sheila, this is ridiculous. How can a man get pregnant?" I hoped it would throw her off the scent. It didn't.

"I think you know perfectly well that Jordan has lady parts. What I don't get is how you can carry a baby in your penis."

I was outraged. "I don't know where you get your information, Sheila, but it's completely false!" I slammed the phone down. It rang several more times, but I didn't answer it.

When Jordan got home, I told him what had happened.

He shrugged. "They have no proof. Can they even print it?"

I rolled my eyes. "Freedom of the press is protected. They can say whatever they want. We can only sue if they lied."

I was right, of course. The following day, a paparazzi photo of the two of us coming out of UCLA Medical was on the front page of the Los Angeles Times with the headline "Two Pregnant Men!"

The article was sympathetic but invasive.

Los Angeles, CA

It's a medical miracle. Two men, one biologically male and one trans man, have fathered not one but two children. And no, the trans man is not having twins. The biologically male partner has "Ectopic Phallogeniasis" or Penile Pregnancy.

This reporter spoke to Milo, who confirmed his husband Jordan was pregnant. Though he vehemently denied his own pregnancy, this reporter has medical proof that he has the incredibly rare condition Ectopic Phallogeniasis.

Understandably, Milo declined to elaborate further on his condition or that of his husband. While this is a private matter, it is also a medical marvel that deserves to be celebrated. We hope that in the coming weeks, Milo and Jordan will share their journey with our readers.

—Sheila Spade

Jordan was furious. He vowed to find and kill the reporter. He is way more butch than me. I waited for the anger to subside and then spoke with him level-headedly.

"Jordan, the cat's out of the bag. We can't keep our secret because it's been blown. We need to strategize. Killing Sheila is a terrible plan."

Jordan fumed. "I know. I know, but it's fucking ridiculous. We're gonna be zoo animals now!"

"I think we need to take the bull by the horns."

Sheila's number was in every answering machine message she had left the day before. I called her up and invited her for an interview at the loft.

Sheila Spade brought a photographer and a tape recorder. She didn't want to miss anything. I asked her to be respectful and use euphemisms where possible because the conception was anything but immaculate. She promised to be discreet.

I told her about the sex, how my dick was so long that it stretched the cervix and encouraged an egg to drop. The egg was carried to my bladder because I had hit a wall at the bottom of Jordan's vagina, and the ejaculation reversed and carried it there.

"How did Jordan get pregnant if your ejaculation went in reverse?"

"I come a lot. The first three squirts were retrograde, but the rest came out and impregnated Jordan."

I squeezed his shoulder. The photographer got a good picture of the two of us.

Jordan broke his silence. "I didn't become a man to be a mother, but now that I have life growing inside me, I get it. Motherhood or fatherhood, either way, I'm proud to carry a child. And I'm proud that Milo is carrying mine."

The next day's paper carried a respectful article about the two of us. It was syndicated, and I started hearing about some unfriendly rewrites in the Bible Belt.

One headline read, "Satanist Freaks Father Twins." Another said, "Perverts Plan to Raise Their Spawn."

Of course, Sally Jesse Raphael and Phil Donahue wanted us to be on their shows. We had trouble leaving the apartment because of all the paparazzi out to get a shot of the "freak festival."

The most embarrassing part for me was the way my pregnancy showed. I couldn't wear anything but the loosest sweatpants, and even then, the bulge was obscene. Most of the news photographs of me were blurred from the waist down.

Despite my cock having swollen to the size of a goat, I was still able to urinate and ejaculate. The baby gave off hormones that made my cock looser and stretchier than a pair of Lycra running shorts. It was ironic I couldn't run, even if I needed to. And I needed to.

❧ 7 ❧

TAKEN

Leaving the loft one day in our seventh month, a black van pulled up. Four men built like gorillas rushed us and handcuffed us. They put burlap bags over our heads and shoved us in. The only sound I heard was the purring of the motor and the clicks of the many shutters capturing the event. Not one paparazzo tried to help us. They just recorded the kidnapping, knowing their pictures were worth thousands. If they foiled the kidnapping, they would be worth mere hundreds. "Help!" I screamed loud enough for someone at the beach to hear.

Then, a strong chemical smell put me to sleep. What little light that came through the bag on my head faded to black.

When I came to, we were on the open highway.

"Where are you taking us?"

Nobody answered. "Come on, what's happening? Please?"

Jordan shushed me, whispering. "They'll just knock you out again. Stay quiet."

The men said very little. At one point, the guy said, "Towards Lone Pine, not Tehachapi." From that, I deduced we were going to drive East in the High Desert.

Jordan and I feigned sleep in hopes that we would

catch more information. They bought it and spoke in whispers.

"Chief's not going to like that you chloroformed the dude."

"I had to shut him up."

"It was stupid and dangerous for the baby."

So, we knew there was a Chief, and he was interested in keeping our children alive. Much of the whispering was too soft. But I heard some valuable landmarks.

"No, Death Valley. Take the Right fork."

The van was unbearably hot. We were in Death Valley, headed East.

The last thing I managed to hear was "Amargosa." I knew Amargosa was in the same county where the nuclear tests took place. There were lots of secret tunnels, underground bunkers, and CIA strongholds in the area.

I whispered to Jordan, "CIA. I think."

Jordan said, "Yeah. You're right."

And I was right.

❧ 8 ❧

CENTRAL INTELLIGENCE

We were in a windowless bunker when the bags came off our heads. The thugs walked us to an office where a man who looked like Colonel Sanders was chattering on the phone.

"Oh, they're here. Yeah, gotta go."

He turned to us. "Welcome. I'm sorry for the rather brutal extraction, but we needed to be sure you didn't try to leave."

Jordan's temper flared. "Who the fuck are you, and where the fuck are we?"

Colonel Sanders said, "I'm Colonel McCool. You're at a CIA hospital about an hour from Las Vegas."

I said, "Why are we here, sir?"

"Quite frankly, you're here because you need our protection. Since we first learned about you, we've had men on the ground monitoring your safety. Yesterday, we foiled a bombing in your building. Some religious extremists are denouncing your children as the Antichrist."

I had more questions. "Well, thanks, but why a kidnapping in plain sight? What are you going to tell the press?"

Colonel McCool smiled. "You probably didn't get a chance to see the side of the van. Go have a look."

I walked back to the van and saw it was painted with the name of a church in Kansas. Then I understood.

When I returned to the office, Jordan was in a heated argument.

He said, "I didn't realize we were in danger. Thank you. But can we go back to our fucking lives now?"

I said, "No, Jordan, we can't. We have to tell the world a sad story and vanish."

Colonel McCool nodded. "Your husband is right. We can't let one of the most important scientific advances in human history be silenced by religion or bombs."

I was used to thinking of the CIA as a bunch of Machiavellian evildoers, but I was seeing the other side of that coin. They wanted to protect us because we were national treasures.

Jordan needed convincing. "What makes us important?"

The colonel said, "Before you two impregnated each other, we knew almost nothing. We didn't know if a trans man would be able to produce milk, which, sadly, you cannot. And we had no idea how Ectopic Phallogeniasis would affect the biological male's health. All prior cases were among men with small to average penises and ended with termination in the second month. There was a case with a guy well above average, but sadly, we had to excise the fetus in the fourth month."

I realized my good fortune. "So, you're saying my whopper cock is why this baby is surviving?"

"Precisely. You're not big; you're enormous. And we need to study your genome to determine what combination of genes caused your penis to grow so excessively large. If we're going to colonize planets, we need everyone reproducing. You're the key." It all came together. We're part of the space race. It was kind of cool, although I didn't appreciate being kidnapped.

Colonel McCool clapped his hands, and two gorilla men saluted.

"Take them to their suite. I'm sure they're exhausted."

The men walked us to an elevator. I noted we were on floor -11. He punched -18, and the elevator descended further into the earth. It was noticeably warmer on the negative eighteenth floor.

The CIA had spared no expense in furnishing our rooms. We had a kitchenette with a Sub-Zero refrigerator and an AGA stove. The living room was sleek and modern. Behind the curtains, artificial sunlight glowed. We fell into the most comfortable king-sized bed I've ever experienced, and we both drifted into a long, dreamless sleep.

The most significant advantage of living in a state-of-the-art CIA facility was that the hospital came to you. No traffic, no delays. To our annoyance, we had doctors and nurses poking and prodding us at all hours of the day. The greatest disadvantage was the sheer boredom of living in a gilded dungeon. We had cable television, radio, newspapers - everything the CIA could find to keep us connected to the world at large.

We watched the sad story of our kidnappings unfold on the nightly news. The Apostles of the Church of the Seventh Son were responsible for our demise. Two bodies, badly burned, were found in a Kansas rest area. "Medical reports" confirmed that they were us. We were gone.

Jordan's parents probably didn't shed a tear. They were mortally ashamed of him. They would be glad that the Jesus freaks took him out.

I was an orphan, so I had only my friends to mourn me. They organized a candlelight vigil for Jordan and me in Pershing Square. The Westboro Baptist Church, another Kansas anti-fag church, came and picketed. The folks with candles chased them off.

My cock had become too large for even the tiniest

bit of anal sex with Jordan. Jordan was going through hormonal changes that left him frigid. He didn't miss it. On the other hand, I was crawling the walls wishing they had a bathhouse on floor negative seventeen.

Of the four gorillas who kidnapped us, one was handsome. He had sandy blond hair and green eyes. I found myself staring at his hulking form, wondering what was underneath that suit. To my surprise, he returned my stare with a smile.

"Archie." He extended a hand. I reddened as we shook.

"Nice to meet you, Archie." I was so horny and desperate; I couldn't keep my eyes above his waist.

"Take a picture, it'll last longer." He grabbed a significant lump in his pants and adjusted it. It appeared to be growing.

"You need some help with that?"

He chuckled. "They got cameras all over the place. Meet me on negative fourteen at 9 pm. That's got a big janitor's closet. They all go home by then."

I could barely keep still at dinner. Jordan noticed me fidgeting.

"Milo, you okay?"

"Yeah, I'm just a little restless. I'm going to explore the facility after dinner."

And while I explored the facility, it explored me back.

❀ 10 ❀

ARCHIE

At 9 pm, I found the janitor's closet. Archie was inside waiting for me. He loosened his tie and unbuttoned his white shirt, revealing a wife beater underneath. His arms were like sculpted marble. Every muscle was out and on display. When he took off his pants and folded them neatly, I watched the muscles at work. His nipples jumped with each fold.

"I gotta kiss when I fuck. Okay?"

I nodded, counting my blessings. He pressed his lips into mine, and I could feel his cock hardening against my leg. He took off his BVDs, revealing his substantial swollen member and a dimpled ass that jutted out like a bookshelf. He was so strong, he lifted me up and held me close. I wrapped my legs around his waist.

With the spit from our kiss, he lubed up my hole and his cock. I put my hands on his pectoral muscles and played with his nipples. He nearly dropped me. My baby-swollen cock dangled down, blocking my hole. Archie gently moved it aside and pushed his head against my hole until it popped in.

It had been so long that I was out of practice. I shrieked.

"Oh god, I'm sorry Milo. Did I hurt you?"

I shook my head. "Fuck me."

Archie was an animal. He pounded me hard while carrying me around the big closet until he found a counter to set me down. He raised one of my legs and fucked me from the side. Despite the baby blockade, my cock still produced prostate juice, which trickled down and landed on the counter. Archie fucked with all his muscles. I marveled as they rippled with each thrust. I couldn't see his ass, but my hand confirmed that it, too, was fully engaged in the act of sex.

"Rub my ass, man."

It was a little awkward, but I managed to hold his ass in one hand and pull him close while he humped me. I licked my finger and took a risk. I pushed the tip of my finger past his hole.

"Yeah! Oh god, Milo. Keep going."

I massaged Archie's prostate, feeling the increased lubrication from the pre-cum. The more I pushed, the more slippery my hole got.

Archie kissed me passionately, causing me to release another stream of pre-cum. And when I felt his abdominal muscles ripple like a corrugated tin washboard, I got too excited.

"Oh fuck, I'm gonna…" I didn't get to finish the sentence. My bloated cock spit out a geyser of cum. It soiled the countertop.

"Oh fuck, no hands. That's so hot." Archie pounded harder, pushing the last drops of my cum out with the pressure of his big tool inside me.

"I'm coming!" He tensed up so that every muscle in his body was as rock hard as his cock, then released, flooding my ass with his cum. He stayed inside me, throbbing, until there was too much in me, and it began to leak out past his cock. He pulled back, releasing the tidal flow of his juices. They cascaded down my leg and puddled on the floor.

I turned to face Archie, and we kissed until he got

hard again. The second round was just as intense and lasted longer.

When we were getting dressed, I felt something like a band-aid taken from my skin. Archie had removed an electrode. It turned out our tryst wasn't just a good time. Archie had been tasked with taking readings of my vitals to find out the effects of anal sex during the third trimester of Ectopic Phallogeniasis. It was then I realized this was no dungeon. I was a lab rat in a gilded maze.

11

IN TROUBLE

The next night at dinner, collecting our salad plates, Archie dropped a tightly folded napkin onto my dinner plate. Nobody saw as I ferreted it away in the pocket of my robe. Back at our little underground lair, I opened the napkin in the bathroom.

It said, "I need more. Same place. Same time. Chow."

I chuckled at his attempt at Italian. Jordan was watching Mary Tyler Moore, so he scarcely noticed me slip out.

Back on the 14th floor, I waited in the closet. Archie appeared and shut the door. A bare bulb cast shadows in the corners of our faces and the room. He kissed me passionately, holding my head in his big meaty paws.

"Fuck, Milo, you're so fucking hot." I glanced down and saw Archie's magnificent cock straining against the brown double-knit polyester fabric of his pants. The head was outlined perfectly, and it throbbed. I fumbled with his buckle until the pants came undone, falling to the floor. Archie was at full mast.

"What are you measuring this time?"

Archie grinned. "This is off the books."

I had never sucked cock before. I never realized how hard it was to do it right. Archie held me by my ears and pressed as far back as he could. It was about halfway in. I gagged. Archie stood still until my retching subsided.

"Open your throat like you need to cough."

I tried. He pushed hard but couldn't get past my tonsils. My eyes watered as I gagged some more. But it wasn't as bad as the first time. He persisted, just pressing hard and releasing. Suddenly, with an internal 'pop,' the head slipped past the tonsils. He pressed hard, forcing himself deeper into my esophagus. I needed air. I pulled my head back and cleared my airway. I took a giant gasp. Without waiting, Archie pushed his way back in until his balls hit my chin. Then he pivoted back and forth, fast, fucking my face.

I was immensely pleased with myself for having mastered such a difficult sex act in one try. Archie patted my cheek and said, "Good boy."

My cock had come to life, so I stroked it idly, rubbing the tip against my chin. Archie grasped it and used it to balance while he rocked in and out of my face. Every time the balls hit my chin, they smacked the head of my cock, too. It felt like victory.

"Show me that sweet ass, Milo."

I rotated and kneeled, ass up. Archie whistled. "Fuck that's a sweet hole you got."

I spread my cheeks and felt his spit-slippery cock force its way into my shitter. The pathway he opened yesterday was still there, and he could fill me completely, passing the second hole.

"Oh, shit, that feels good. Oh shit. I'm gonna come."

My oral skills had prepared him too well. He came in several thick spurts. My insides grew warm.

"Who's there?" A voice called from outside the closet door.

Before we could even separate, Colonel McCool opened the door.

"The test was yesterday, Sergeant."

Archie blushed. "Yes, sir."

The colonel stepped close. "You're in a buttload of trouble, young man."

He wasn't talking to me.

Archie said, "Sir, please. I can't."

The colonel whipped off his belt and lowered his slacks, exposing a huge, hard, fat cock. It wasn't as long as Archie's but twice as thick. Thick enough to carry a baby, probably.

The colonel came behind Archie and grabbed his waist.

"You know the punishment, Archie."

There was a loud cry. I don't think Archie was ready for anything that big. I heard the colonel spit several times and then another loud cry. It repeated a few times until, at last, the Colonel said, "Ohhh, yeah."

He grabbed Archie by the hips and thrust, forcing Archie deeper into my already sloppy hole.

"Fuck!!" Archie may have been protesting, but his throbbing cock in my hole told a different story. He liked it. Our trio arrived at a rhythm that allowed Archie to slide forward into me and back onto the Colonel's cock at an even pace.

Getting fucked was nice, but Archie was the luckiest. He got to fuck and be fucked at the same time.

The Colonel let out a series of grunts. "I'm gonna come in you, boy."

Archie said, "Come in me, sir."

"Aaargh!" The Colonel sounded like a pirate. I heard wet droplets explode out of Archie's ass and spatter on the ground. It was so hot, it put me over.

"I'm gonna come," I warned.

Archie said, "Wait, wait for me. I'm almost there."

I hovered on the edge of orgasm with my cock in

hand while Archie probed me deeply over and over in rapid strokes. I let my cock go and watched in fascination as it exploded in perfect sync with Archie's hot spurts inside me.

The Colonel whistled. "Hands-free. Good work, young men. Now clean up this mess."

The mess was only half mine. The rest was the Colonel's cum that met no resistance as it left Archie's stretched-out gaping hole. Archie's cum was all inside me, and I held it there, savoring the feeling. I could poop it out later.

"You're pregnant. Let me clean." Archie got a pail of warm water and some rags and cleaned up the cum stains from the linoleum. When he was done, he turned to me, serious.

"I want you to myself. The Colonel tore me apart just now. But we can't meet. He'll find us here."

"Let me talk to Jordan. We can probably work something out."

12

SHARE AND SHARE ALIKE

The following day, I told Jordan about what had been going on.

"Let's have him over for dinner. You can get some privacy that way."

Jordan was not the jealous type at all. Still, his generosity was more than human. He just wanted people to be happy. Sex was off the table for him, but I was a dog in heat. There is no sense in being jealous or torturing one another by withholding sex or forcing it on the other. The middle path was clear. Archie would fuck me in our bedroom while Jordan watched his shows in the living room.

When dinner time rolled around, Jordan cooked our favorite: stuffed bell peppers. He made a leek and potato soup for a starter. Archie came in his civilian clothes - a tight polo shirt, jeans, and sneakers. He looked like a tennis player on steroids. His muscles strained the fabric of the shirt, highlighting his hard nipples.

Jordan had trouble keeping his eyes from straying. Archie caught him more than once and grinned. "Like what you see?" Jordan blushed. When the bell peppers came out of the oven, the temperature in the room rose with the sexual tension.

I felt pangs of jealousy as Jordan made butterfly eyes at the hunky blond guard. But the green-eyed monster grew calm as I thought about the possibilities opening up.

Jordan had been uninterested in sex for months, but Archie's manly aroma had awoken something. How could this work?

I found out immediately after dinner. Jordan had planned to make crepes for dessert, but the plans evaporated when Archie took off his shirt, revealing the golden-brown chest with hairy nipples and deltoids to beat Charles Atlas.

Jordan whistled. "Holy crap! You're built like a brick shithouse."

Archie winked at me, then said, "Wait until you see what I got downstairs."

The next few minutes were a blur of discarded clothing, passionate kisses, groping hands, and hard cocks. We were in the bedroom. Jordan lay on his back, his vagina spread wide to allow Archie easy entry. He pressed in easily, coming to a halt at the shallow bottom of Jordan's pussy. It was deep enough for him. He continued to pump his cock into her pregnant body. I watched in fascination as his ass muscles bulged with each thrust. He had the kind of butt you only ever saw in a dirty bookstore magazine.

Jordan moaned softly. "Oh shit. Oh, that feels so good." His hands caressed the swollen muscles and found their way to the firm buttocks. He pressed Archie in as deep as nature allowed.

I got behind Archie and clamped my mouth over his hole. It was extremely loose. Apparently, he and the Colonel had been busy for a long time. I wondered if he could handle the first few inches of my swollen pregnant cock. Now that he was lubed up with my spit, I figured trying couldn't hurt.

The head slipped in easily. He was one of the loosest

asses I'd ever fucked. He was flexible enough to allow the entire length of my cock in right up until it reached the baby. I didn't want to crush my unborn child, so I didn't force myself any further, but I probably could have.

Archie did all the work. He fucked forward into Jordan's pussy and pushed back onto my throbbing hardon. Jordan cupped his big balls and squeezed them gently. I reached forward and pinched both Archie's nipples between my fingers. He buckled for a moment. They were a weak spot. I leaned around his side and licked one of the nipples. He bucked and nearly pulled off of my dick. Jordan cried out because Archie had punched the cervix.

"Sorry. I'm just so sensitive! But I like it. Don't stop."

I twisted and licked his nipples while he fucked himself onto my heavy dick. Jordan put his feet on Archie's hips and wriggled, jiggling the fat cock inside his pussy.

Jordan had a female orgasm like only he could. He moaned and thrashed and asked for more. Archie obliged. His thrusts and pushes made my cock quiver. At last, I could take no more.

"Shit, I'm coming."

I filled Archie with my sperm until it overflowed and ran down his meaty thighs. I saw him reach down, scoop a little, sniff it, and then eat it.

I think a pregnant man's cum must be full of crazy hormones because Archie went wild. He pounded Jordan, bringing on orgasm after orgasm. Jordan pulled me close and put my dick in his mouth like a greedy cock hungry whore. He sucked out the juices left from my first orgasm and didn't stop until I fed him another. It took a while. Every few minutes, Jordan would stop and cry out as another orgasm rocked his body.

"Can I come in you?" Archie didn't need to ask.

Jordan held his waist and helped bring him to orgasm. He gushed so hard; I could hear the liquid fighting to coexist with his mammoth cock inside Jordan's sloppy hole. When he pulled out, a stream of cum trickled out onto the bedspread.

And so, Archie revived our marriage. But as much as he saved our sex life, he put the rest of our lives in real danger.

13

BUSTED

We were lab rats in a dark operation. Nobody outside, other than a few government agents, knew we existed. To the rest of the world, we were kidnapped. Our gilded cage began to tarnish as the weeks rolled on. Archie was the one high-light of our otherwise monotonous existence.

We had worked out a schedule that would be hard to identify to a casual observer. Three days off, two days off, one day off, two days off, three days off. Nobody appeared to put a stop to our sexual liaisons. During the times between, we rested, cooked, walked, and generally grew ever more bored until our blond savior showed up with his fat cock.

One "Archie" night, the knock came, and I threw open the door to see the Colonel with two guards, neither of which was Archie.

"What's up?" I tried to sound nonchalant.

The colonel raised an eyebrow. "Expecting someone else?" We were busted.

Without any warning, the guards forced us into handcuffs and marched us to the elevator. We descended to -31, a level I hadn't even imagined existed.

Colonel McCool spoke on the way down. "This is for your own good. We gave you enough freedom to live a semblance of a life underground. You were expressly forbidden from having sex this late in your pregnancy. Now that you have, many of our tests have to be recalibrated.

Jordan spoke with a hiss. "Where's Archie?"

The Colonel smiled. "I've got him somewhere beyond your reach but well within mine. You fucked with the wrong guard, my friends. Archie is mine."

I said, "So this was a jealous act of revenge."

The Colonel didn't deny it.

Our new home was under lock and key. Two guards were always posted to prevent our escape. The doctors who came to visit were forbidden to engage in conversation. They simply gave orders: "Left arm, hold your breath, lift your penis for me." Their eyes were different, too. Before, they had been engaged and exhilarated to be working with us. Now, there was a deadness behind their eyes.

Life on negative 31 was far worse than the monotony of the negative 18th floor. Literally, the only thing that happened was bi-weekly doctor visits. Someone else prepared our jailhouse meals. We didn't have a television either—only books, which we read voraciously.

One day, a female doctor was palpating the fetus in my dick when out of her sleeve, she produced a slip of paper. I was about to ask what it was, but she shook her head and said, "I'll check the reading when I get back."

The way she said it, I knew it was code: 'Read this after I'm gone.'

I waited twenty minutes or so, then picked up a copy of Brave New World, unfolding the slip of paper inside. In tiny letters, it read, "They plan to kill you when this is over." Suddenly, the dead-eyed doctors made sense. They had to detach from us because we were going into the incinerator when this wrapped up.

"Jordan, have you read Brave New World?"

"No, hon, I don't think so."

"There's a brilliant passage I think you should read." I walked over and pointed. "Here, this is it."

Jordan's face turned gray after reading our death sentence.

My dick was too big to keep in my pants, so the doctors gave me a hospital gown with an open back. Jordan only needed loose sweats and a maternity top. As I paced the jail cell disguised as a studio apartment, my dick swung hard from side to side. It looked and felt like I was carrying a flour sack between my legs.

I didn't know how frequently we were being monitored. I assumed it was 24/7, but maybe they weren't always listening. I needed to have a plain conversation with Jordan and plot our escape. Who knows what happens once one of us gives birth? To get out of a secure CIA compound sounded like a job for Chuck Norris. But we had to try.

That night, after lights out, I whispered to Jordan. "Do you think they're listening?"

"Why?"

I winked. "I'm gonna end it. I'm going to ask the doctor for a pair of scissors, and I'm ending it."

"No! I need you!"

I winked again. "Trust me. It's for the best."

The next day, I pointed out a long, loose thread on my green hospital gown. The doctor had a needle in my arm, drawing blood.

"Can I use your scissors?"

I pointed to a pair of surgical scissors in her vest pocket. She shrugged. I took the scissors, cut the thread, then put them back in her pocket. Nobody tried to stop me! It meant our conversations, whispered at night, were private.

That night, we plotted our escape. It was elaborate. We had both been to the hospital floor before. The plan was to go into false labor simultaneously. They'd wheel us up to the hospital, and from there, we'd find scrubs and masks and get to the outside. We were going to have to be prepared to steal a car. We didn't know if we could rescue Archie, but we had to try. He was a part of our family now. The Colonel was keeping him somewhere. We couldn't leave him.

There were so many "what ifs" to our flimsy plan. What if we couldn't find scrub and masks? What if someone saw the monster in my pants? What if we couldn't find Archie? What if we couldn't leave? What if they figure out what we're up to? How would we find a car? We were going to have to improvise.

14

FALSE LABOR

I decided to wait ten minutes after Jordan to begin my false labor. While they were busy loading him into a gurney, I gave out a scream of pain. "It's coming!"

In the confusion, I managed to snatch a badge from one of the doctors and wedge it in my ass. It hurt a little, but it was the only pocket I had!

They rolled me into a different room from Jordan. It was little more than a bed, a wardrobe, and a night table. I moaned and cried to really sell that this was it.

The nurse said, "We're understaffed. I'll send a doctor, but we only have one obstetrician and urologist on duty." Fine. The obstetrician would figure out the labor was false in almost no time, but the urologist was in uncharted territories. I had more time than Jordan. That meant I had to act fast.

The urologist strolled in. "Big day! New life. How often are the contractions coming?"

"Is that what this is? It feels like a horse stepped on my dick."

The urologist tried to pretend he knew what was happening. "I imagine those are contractions, yes. The embryo is detaching from the urethra. Gravity should help a little. We'll probably need to squeeze you like a tube of toothpaste."

I was grateful to hear any instructions on how to handle the birth when it did come.

I asked the doctor, "Will they let us go home after that?"

The doctor got that dead look in his eyes. He knew there was no life after birth for me. Unlike the kind lady, he didn't want to help. "I'm sure they have a place for you all lined up." He might as well have been a Nazi doctor.

I cried out. "Oh god, please check it, please!" I lifted my gown, revealing my swollen cock, made so much bigger by the late-term embryo.

"Where does it hurt?"

I pointed to the part of my shaft swollen by the un-born child. The doctor took out a stethoscope to listen. I seized the chance. Snatching the stethoscope, I stran-gled him, twisting ever tighter. I didn't want to kill him. As soon as he went limp, I pulled him off me. I quickly stripped him of his clothes and found a mask in his long lab coat pocket. The coat covered my bulge, so it was less conspicuous. I cut a massive hole in the crotch of the pants so I could get them on.

I pulled the unconscious doctor by the shoulders and stuffed him into the wardrobe, tying the door han-dles together with the rubber from the stethoscope.

I walked carefully so as not to swing the baby. With my mask, badge, and long white coat, nobody gave me a second look. I found the obstetrics lab. A nurse was lis-tening to the heartbeat and shaking her head.

"I don't think those are contractions, love. Did you maybe eat something that disagreed with you?"

I said, "Nurse, I need to examine the patient my-self." The nurse frowned, unsure who I was, but she saw the embroidered name followed by 'M.D.' on my lab coat and shrugged. "Shall I tell the obstetrician to come in?"

"No, in fact, ask him to wait."

"Ask HER to wait."

I'd forgotten that the Asian female doctor was the obstetrician. I didn't want her implicated in this. She was the only one who had tried to help us.

I went out on a limb. "Nurse, can you send Archie up here before you go?"

"Archie, the guard?"

I nodded.

"Chief's not gonna like that."

"Do as you're told."

"I don't have a pass card for neg 13."

"Never mind, I'll get someone else to do it."

The nurse shrugged again and strolled out. She was going to talk. She was that kind of busybody.

I had precious few minutes to get us out of there. Jordan was out of the stirrups and digging through the room, looking for scrubs, coats, masks, anything. There was nothing. I decided to take a calculated risk.

"Nurse!"

She poked her head back in.

"Send in the obstetrician. I need her opinion."

A minute went by, and then the Asian doctor came in. She frowned, not recognizing a colleague.

I pulled down the mask and held up a finger. "I need your help."

15

FLAYED ALIVE

The doctor had a good idea. While Jordan swapped clothes and tied her to the birthing table, I made a beeline for the 13th floor. I would gather Archie and meet Jordan near the entrance to the compound. The doctor gave her keys to Jordan.

I wasn't prepared for what I saw on floor negative 13. Archie was chained to the wall, his clothes in tatters from the many lashes of the whip the Colonel gave him. Despite the horror of the situation, I felt myself turned on. My cock began to fill with blood.

"Not now!" I hissed. The monster was rearing its head, making it impossible to hide.

I lowered my mask and smiled. Archie rolled his head, and his eyes lit up. "Milo? How— "

"No time. Where are the keys?"

They were out of reach on a table. I undid Archie's shackles. He was weak. His big cock flopped out from between his legs. I sent him to clean up while I figured out how to get him dressed. There was a wheelchair in the next room and a bed with white sheets. It would look ridiculous, but my doctor's jacket could lend the air of credibility we needed. I wrapped Archie from head to toe in the sheet and buckled him into the wheelchair. He looked like a moth larva on wheels.

Personnel on the elevator frowned and looked like they would ask too many questions, so I headed them off. "Corpse. Chief went overboard. Say farewell to Archie."

The staff were all visibly disturbed by this news. They could see some of Archie's flayed flesh peeking through the sheets. It lent an air of genuine horror.

At floor zero, we ran into trouble beyond what I could imagine. The Colonel, six guards, and the two doctors stood by the entrance. The Colonel held a gun to Jordan's head.

I had nothing to lose.

"Do you know who this is?" I pointed to the bundle of sheets and bloody flesh in the wheelchair. "It's your coworker Archie. Dead. He killed him!" I pointed an accusing finger at the evil Chief of this godforsaken lab.

The six guards were visibly shaken. I continued. "His only crime was he was sexy. The Colonel wanted him for himself. He tortured him. He killed him."

The Colonel bellowed. "He isn't dead!"

Archie didn't stir. I peeled back the sheet, revealing more and more signs of torture at the hands of the Colonel. The guards bought it. Six guns pointed at the Colonel's head.

"He's not dead! See, he breathed."

I said, "Even if he were alive, would you work for someone who could do this to one of your own?"

Heads shook emphatically. The guard closest to the Colonel said, "Let her go."

Jordan said, "I'm a boy. Let him go." Leave it to Jordan to be fussy when being released from bondage.

The other guards chimed in. "Let him go! Let him go!" When the Colonel didn't budge, one fired in the air. The Colonel ducked, and Jordan grabbed the gun, prying it from his hand.

"We don't want any trouble. We're out of here."

The colonel said, "You won't make it one day out there in the desert."

Jordan resisted the urge to dangle keys. Good. The less he knew, the better. "We'll take our chances."

Archie stood, letting the sheet fall away. Nobody could resist stealing a glance at his magnificent cock. He walked over to the Colonel and pulled down his pants. "I'll be taking these." They were too tight, but they covered his lower half, unbuttoned and unzipped though they were.

The guard who first said, "Let her go," smiled at Archie. "Here, take this." He stripped off his shirt and tossed it to the handsome blond. He took out his wallet and removed a few twenties. "For the road, brother."

We headed out the door.

"This is treason!" We heard the Colonel shout. Then, there was a loud report. Turning, I saw the colonel and half his head hit the floor. The other half was atomized. The Asian doctor held a smoking gun in her hand.

She yelled, "Run!"

16

LA TIMES

From the Los Angeles Times
By Sheila Spade
Las Vegas, Nevada

Last week, the pregnant couple escaped from a bunker with a harrowing tale of kidnap, deceit, and governmental treachery.

In the wake of the arrest of the CIA's "Bunker Butcher" Colonel McCool, a story emerged that rivals any Hollywood action flick. Milo and Jordan, who made headlines with their male pregnancies, were 'disappeared' Argentina-style. Although the press release from the FBI blamed a conservative church in Kansas, it was, in fact, Colonel McCool who was behind the operation.

In an exclusive interview, this reporter learned that Jordan and Milo were held captive to be studied at a CIA bunker outside Las Vegas. They said the accommodations were spare but comfortable, and the medical tests were frequent but bearable.

According to Milo, something "snapped" a month ago. He refused to talk about the reasons, but this reporter learned from inside sources that the jealous Colonel became enraged when his private guard, Archie, became involved sexually with the pregnant couple.

The couple were jailed in an escape-proof cell; Archie was imprisoned and tortured. A brave doctor told the couple that they were slated for extermination at the end of the pregnancy. This reporter will not name her for reasons of safety. Milo plotted an elaborate escape, which will be the subject of tomorrow's article. Simply put, it was just as impossible as a man carrying a fetus to term.

Both Jordan and Milo will give birth in a Las Vegas hospital next week. This reporter will be there to cover the miraculous event.

PARTURITION

❧ 17 ❧

PARTURITION

The contractions started at 7 am. Jordan watched helplessly as I screamed with pain. My urethra felt like it was caught in a zipper. All up and down the length of my cock, the corpus cavernosum throbbed in rhythmic pulses, pushing the baby forward. The nurse held the base, squeezed, and pushed. It helped a little, but the pain was too much. I fainted. When I came to, our child was crowning at the head of my penis. I could see the little scalp stretching my pee hole wider than it should ever have been. The little ears popped out one by one, and then, in a swift forward motion, the whole head emerged. It was trapped at the shoulders. The nurse squeezed the giant tube of toothpaste that was my cock, but the infant wouldn't budge.

The doctor said, "We will have to perform an emergency surgery."

I looked at Jordan, who fought back tears.

I said, "Wait! Wait! I can do this." With some effort, I focused on my cremaster muscles and visualized them connecting to muscles that could push the baby out. Any anatomy doctor would tell you this is physically impossible. We have no muscles to speak of in our penis.

But it worked. I bore down like I was forcing out a last droplet of cum, and the baby scooted forward. Once the first shoulder cleared, the doctor grabbed forceps and tugged on the baby while the nurse squeezed from behind. I looked up at the operating theater. I had forgotten there were dozens of medical researchers watching this historic moment.

"It's a girl."

⚜

JORDAN'S BIRTH WAS ALSO HISTORIC BUT NOT AS unusual as my own. The only questions it answered were whether testosterone, while the fetus is in utero, can cause birth defects or other complications in the first eight weeks. It also proved that it had no lasting effect on the hormones that initiate labor. Jordan's birth was textbook normal, with plenty of pain but no complications. He gave birth to a baby boy.

There was some question as to whether the hormones had hyper-masculinized the fetus because it came out, well, very male. There was hair on its chest, and the penis was enormous for an infant. I reminded the researchers that he probably inherited the oversized tool from me.

With the help of the FBI, Jordan, Archie, and I were relocated anonymously to San Diego. We live as a polyamorous trio. We never tire of sex. We recently got great news that Jordan is expecting again. I hauled my massive appendage to the doctor for an ultrasound, but no kids were lurking in there. My cock still got rock hard, even though it had stretched to nearly double the length and width. I guess I just have good genes down there.

There will be some tricky explanations for our kids when they're old enough to understand. For now, we'll focus on helping them appreciate how lucky they are to have three daddies.

ABOUT PETER SCHUTES

Peter Schutes is the nom de plume of a prolific and acclaimed novelist. As Peter Schutes, he is the author of Adult Erotic Fiction such as <u>The Slaves of Rome</u>, <u>Dark as a Dungeon</u>, <u>The Gospel of Priapus</u>, and <u>Panama Heat</u>. He writes in the style of vintage pulp authors from the 1960s and 1970s. He lives in Los Angeles.

OTHER BOOKS FROM PETER SCHUTES PUBLISHING

Please visit peterschutes.com to find links to all of Peter's books.

E-books and Paperbacks

The Able Seaman

The Anaconda Copper

The Autobiography of Peter Schutes

Backwoods Delivery

Big Bodies of All Sizes

Big Hole River

Bobbing Buoys and Salty Seamen

Buck Private

Bunkhouse Buddies

The Butt Baby

Chopper Jock

Cloistered

Coached

Confessions of a Rodeo Clown

Cosmic Cage

Dark as a Dungeon

Demonic Deception *aka* Deceived, Cursed & Blessed

Desert Island Daddies

Dirty Dorms and Fresh Men

Dormitory Urges

Dutch Treat

The Expectant Member

Under the Boardwalk

Wee Dobbin

World's Biggest

***** Coming Soon *****

Come Young and Old

More Tales of Two Daddies

Mowing and Blowing